DETROIT PUBLIC LIBRARY
P9-ASH-239

KiKi Swinson
NEW YORK TIMES BEST SELLING AUTHOR
Wifey's
Next
TWISTED FATE
DETROIT PUBLIC LIBRARY

This is a work of fiction. All of the characters, organizations, and events portrayed in this novel are either products of the author's imagination or are used fictitiously.

Publisher's address:

K.S. Publications
P.O. Box 68878
Virginia Beach, VA 23471

Website: www.kikiswinson.net
Email: KS.publications@yahoo.com

ISBN-13: 978-0986203732
ISBN-10: 0986203734

First Edition: December 2016

10 9 8 7 6 5 4 3 2 1

Editors: Letitia Carrington
Interior & Cover Design: Davida Baldwin (OddBalldsgn.com)
Cover Photo: Davida Baldwin

Printed in the United States of America

Don't Miss Out On These Other Titles:

Wifey
I'm Still Wifey
Life After Wifey
Still Wifey Material
Wifey 4-Life
Wife Extraordinaire
Wife Extraordinaire Returns
Wife Extraordinaire Reloaded
Wifey's Next Hustle
Wifey's Next Deadly Hustle part 2
Wifey's Next Come Up part 3
The Candy Shop
Still Candy Shopping
A Sticky Situation
Playing Dirty
Notorious
Murder Was The Case
New York's Finest
Internationally Known (New York Finest 2)
I'm Forever New York's Finest (part 3)
Cheaper to Keep Her part 1
Cheaper to Keep Her part 2
Cheaper to Keep Her part 3
Cheaper to Keep Her part 4
Cheaper to Keep Her part 5
Green Eye Bandit part 1
Green Eye Bandit part 2
Ericka Kane
The Score

Novella Collaborations:

Sleeping with the Enemy (with Wahida Clark)
Heist (with De'nesha Diamond)
Heist part 2 (with De'nesha Diamond)
Life Styles of the Rich and Shameless (with Noire)
A Gangster and a Gentleman (with De'nesha Diamond)
Most Wanted (with Nikki Turner)

Another Round of Interrogations

"If someone else gets murdered I am going to have a freaking heart attack!" I screamed after I called my attorney Mr. Kessler and his voicemail picked up. *You've reached the law offices of Kessler, Puloski, and Lancaster please leave your name, number and the nature of your call and someone will get back with you. Have a great day!* "Mr. Kessler, this is Kira Wade, Detective Grimes, his partner and two other cops are standing outside my front door asking me and Dylan to come down to the police station to give a formal statement about another freaking murder. You told me not to speak with any of them if you're not present. Please call me back or meet me at the precinct." I said and then I disconnected the line.

Dylan walked to the back of the apartment. I wasn't sure what he was doing but when I heard the water running from the bathroom sink, my thoughts began to spiral out of control. I rushed to the bathroom door and tried to open it but it was locked. "Dylan, open the door." I whispered softly, but in an urgent manner.

"Give me a second." He replied.

"No, open it now." I wouldn't back down.

"I said, give me a second." He stood his ground.

But I wasn't going for it so I continued to turn the doorknob while I urged him to open the door. "Dylan, what are you doing in there?" I uttered loud enough for only he and I to hear. Well, that's what I thought at least. Out the corner of my right eye Detective Grimes appeared with his partner Detective Brady and snatched me out of the way of the bathroom door. "Hey Dylan, what are you doing in there?" Detective Grimes roared and then he used his left shoulder to force the bathroom door open. After Detective Grimes rushed inside Detective Brady followed. I couldn't see what was going on at first because they tagged teamed me by pushing me out of their way, but as soon as I turned back around I saw that Grimes and Brady had Dylan pinned against the bathroom wall. I moved in closer towards them while Dylan resisted a little. His pants were unzipped while the water from the faucet attached to the sink was running. "Y'all motherfuckers need to get the fuck off me!" Dylan roared.

"Y'all don't have to grab him like that. You see he was trying to use the fucking bathroom!" I spat. The blood flowing through my veins started boiling over.

"Using the bathroom my ass! Looks to me and Brady like he was trying to wash the gun power from his hands." Detective Grimes scoffed as he placed the handcuffs around Dylan's wrists.

"Oh so now y'all trying to pin Bruce's murder on me?" Dylan asked sarcastically as both detectives escorted him out of the bathroom.

"That's some bullshit!" I snapped. "Didn't y'all say it looked like Bruce committed suicide?" I continued as I walked behind them.

Detective Grimes nor Brady attempted to answer my question. "Are y'all arresting me?" Dylan wanted to know.

"No you haven't been formally arrested." Grimes replied after he made Dylan sit down on the living room sofa handcuffed.

"Well, if you haven't arrested him then why the hell does he still have on those handcuffs?" I pressed the issue.

"Yeah, if I haven't been arrested then take these motherfuckers off me." Dylan argued.

By this time, the traffic cops had entered into my apartment with their backs facing the front door while it was slightly ajar. "You better shut up before we hauled your ass through the lobby of this building and show your neighbors that you just can't seem to keep yourself out of trouble."

"Why are y'all fucking harassing us?" I belted out. These fucking cops were getting underneath my skin.

"Why don't you grab your house keys and come with us down to the precinct." Grimes said matter of factly.

"Not until you take the cuffs off my fiancé." I demanded.

"Do you want to end up in cuffs too?" Brady interjected cynically.

I stood there as if I was standing my ground. I knew that these donut-eating fuckers were violating our civil rights and they needed to know that I knew it.

Detective Grimes looked at both of the cops in uniform. Officer Vass, slap the cuffs on her too since she doesn't want to cooperate with us."

"You better not touch her!" Dylan shouted while Officer Vass started walking towards me.

"And what are you going to do about it?" Grimes asked with a smirk on his face.

"Don't touch her!" Dylan threatened.

I looked at Dylan and then I looked back at Officer Vass as my heart started pounding uncontrollably. All I could think about was how these cops were going to make it their business to humiliate Dylan and I if I didn't do what they told me to do. "You fucking bastards!" I huffed and marched over to the table in my foyer, which was only three feet away from me. I grabbed both my handbag and my keys as soon as I came within arms distance of the table. I stood next to the table and gave Detective Grimes and Officer Vass the look of death. "I'm ready." I hissed. I was seething on the inside of my body. I hated that these crooked ass cops had Dylan and I by the balls.

"Good girl." Grimes applauded loudly like he was making a spectacle out of Dylan and I. Then he turned his focus towards

Detective Brady. "Help me get him up on his feet." Detective Grimes instructed him.

"Please take your time with him so y'all won't hurt his wrists." I begged.

"He's a big boy, trust me he can handle it." Grimes continued with his dry humor. I was getting angrier by the second.

"Are you really gonna make me walk pass my neighbors with these fucking cuffs on?" Dylan asked.

"Don't tell me you're worried about being humiliated." Grimes commented after he and Brady lifted Dylan to his feet.

"That's not the point. Remember you said he wasn't arrested." I blurted out.

Brady started unlocking the cuffs while I stood there and watched. I felt a sense of relief when I noticed they were taking the handcuffs off Dylan. I'm sure Dylan did too. After Detective Grimes removed the handcuffs, Dylan began to rub both of his wrists as he let out a sigh of relief. "If everyone is ready let's head on out of here." Detective Grimes said as he pointed towards the front door.

Both police officers led the way out of our apartment, while Dylan and I followed suit. Detective Grimes and Detective Brady exited last. "Whose gonna lock the door?" Detective Brady asked as he looked at Dylan and I.

"I'm gonna lock the door." I replied and then I moved towards the front door. Immediately after I locked it, I turned back around and looked at all four, donut-eating, wanna-be cops and waited for one of them to lead the way. Without saying a word, Officer Vass walked away first, while the rest of us followed. Dylan and I stared at each other the entire elevator ride down to the first floor. I knew he wanted to tell me something by his facial expression. But he knew that now wasn't the right time to do it. "If I didn't know any better, I'd think that you two were sending each other coded messages." Detective Grimes commented while the elevator was carrying us down to the 1st floor.

"And why would we do that?" I interjected.

"It's obvious that you two have secrets. I mean, a lot of bodies are turning up around the city and they are all pointing back to you two." Detective Grimes continued. But before I could entertain his accusations, the elevator door opened.

"Saved by the bell." I blurted out and then I walked off the elevator.

While Dylan and I were escorted through the lobby area of our apartment building, a couple of the residents gawked at us like they were watching a freak show. I was feeling a huge burden of embarrassment. With the constant harassment from the police department, it wouldn't surprise me if the residents in this building vote to have Dylan and I evicted. It wouldn't bother Dylan, but it sure as hell would bother me. In my eyes, this was my home and I wanted to keep it that way.

As soon as we exited the building, I noticed that both of the police vehicles were parked only a few feet away from the valet area. It didn't take long for these assholes to usher me into one car while Dylan was ushered into the other one. Detective Grimes acted like he had all the sense in the world. I knew what he was doing by separating us. But whether he knew it or not, Dylan wasn't going to open his mouth, no matter what questions they tried to ask him and neither was I.

Taking Another Trip Downtown

DYLAN

These fucking cops got some huge balls busting up in my bathroom like they did. I can guarantee that if Kira wasn't in the apartment things would've gotten really ugly. And then to walk Kira and I out of our apartment building with the intentions to embarrass us in front of the staff and our neighbors hit me below the belt. Whether Detective Grimes knew it or not, I was going to off him and his partner Brady as soon as I get the opportunity. And they aren't going to see me coming either.

When we arrived at the police station, the morons took me into one room and took Kira into another one. I guess, they thought that if they separated us they would be able to pressure us into talking. The only thing I wanted to talk about was what time they were going to let me out of here so I could find out what was going on with my mother and my sister. Sitting here in this cold ass room got me to thinking about how cold this world is. My mother was the sweetest woman in the world. She would take strangers off the street and bring them into her house so she could feed them a hot meal. She had a heart of gold. My sister Sonya was a beautiful person too. All she ever wanted to do was become a nurse so she could help people. So why take them from this world when they were ones who made a difference? I swear, everyone who does me wrong is going to pay for my family's death. No one will ever get off easy again. I put that on my life.

After sitting in this room for 30 minutes, Detective Grimes and Detective Brady decided to join me. "Mr. Callender, are you ready to talk to us?" Detective Grimes asked after he took a seat in the chair across from me. Detective Brady stood by the door.

"Don't waste my time. You know I don't have shit to say to neither one of you fake ass cops." I huffed.

Detective Grimes laughed and then he looked at his partner. "He's a funny guy, huh?"

"Yeah, he is." Detective Brady smiled.

"Look, if you're gonna arrest me then arrest me. If you're not then let me go because I have a lot of shit to do." I told them.

"We'll let you go when we're ready to let you go." Detective Grimes said. At one point he started looking demonic. But when I blink my eyes, that demonic looking face disappeared.

"I'll tell you what, since you wanna waste my time let's talk about how you two idiots suck at being cops." I suggested.

"No, let's talk about why are all these bodies dropping around you and your girlfriend?"

"I don't know what you're talking about."

"Come on now Mr. Callender, let's not play games. Do I have to go down the list?"

"It's not gonna matter anyway you look at it."

"Well, I figured if I do a role call, it might jog your memory." Detective Grimes said. "So, lets start with Judge Mahoney and his wife, then it was your girlfriend's co-worker. Am I getting warm?" He asked and then he paused. He looked at his partner Brady and then he started up again, "Ironically, your girlfriend's father was just murdered a few days ago and I'm 100% positive you ordered that hit. I'm just curious as to why your girlfriend did it? Did she want you out of jail that bad that she'd sacrifice her father's life for your freedom? And let's no forget your sister, your mother and her husband. I have a strong feeling that after your mother's husband killed her and your sister, you murdered him and made it look like a suicide. Now tell me if I'm right or wrong?"

"I think you're fucking crazy!"

"So, you aren't denying that you were involved in some way with those murders?" Detective Grimes pressed the issue.

"Look man, I don't have anything else to say to you. Call my lawyer and he'll answer any questions you may have for him."

"You know if you cooperate with us, you could come out on top?"

"What don't you understand when I say I'm not talking to you? I don't have any information for you or him. Arrest me or leave me the fuck alone!" I snapped. These guys were getting on my last nerve. If I could get away with it, I would've smacked one of their asses by now.

"Will you let us test your hands for gunpowder residue?" Detective Brady asked me.

"Yeah, let's do it." I replied.

"He's only allowing us to do it because he already had a chance to wash his hands before we busted the bathroom to restrain him." Detective Grimes pointed out.

"Look man, you can believe what you want." I said as I turned around to look at Detective Grimes and then I turned back around to look at Detective Brady.

Detective Brady looked at Detective Grimes for a few seconds and then he turned his focus towards me. He hesitated and then he stepped away from the door and said, "Let's see what happens."

I stood up from the chair and walked out of the room after Detective Brady opened the door. Detective Grimes followed suit.

Was It Really A Suicide?

KIRA

Once again I found myself down at the police precinct being questioned by these fucking idiots that want me behind bars extremely bad. It had literary become an obsession for Detective Grimes, which is why I had to hire my attorney. So as I sat in the interview room, refusing to answer any of these motherfucking questions, I wondered which interview room they were holding Dylan in and who had Detective Grimes appointed to interrogate him. I knew if I asked Detective Grimes any questions about Dylan, he would shoot it down so I figured why bother?

"Are you going to continue sitting here like you don't know what's going on?" Detective Grimes asked me.

"How many times do I have to tell you that I am not speaking to anyone unless my attorney is here?" I said.

"Okay. You don't have to say another word. But I know you had something to do with your father's murder. And I know that your husband-to-be had something to do with his stepfather's murder. I mean, why else would he come home and watch the gunpowder off hands?" Detective Grimes pointed out.

As bad as I wanted to admit that Detective Grimes made a good point, I refused to side with him. My loyalty was to Dylan, not this prick sitting before me. "You know you are harassing me right?" I finally said.

"You can call it what you want. But I'm on to you and your fiancé. You are a murderer and so is he. And if I don't do anything else, I will make it my business to lock you two crooks up. And after we convict you, I will make sure the judge gives you both the death penalty." He said and then he stood up from his chair and exited the room.

A lot of people would be intimidated when they are in a room by themselves, surrounded by crackers with badges, but I'm not. This is not my first or second time going toe to toe with a room full of cops. I know how to deal with them. So does Dylan, which is why they are trying to make our lives a living hell. Whether they know it or not, my man and I will fight this to the end. End of story.

After Detective Grimes left the interview room, I laid my head down on the cold, iron table and closed my eyes. I tried my hardest to clear my mind of everything going on around me, but I couldn't. The fact that Detective Grimes was trying to pen Bruce's death on Dylan was mind-boggling. I knew Dylan hated Bruce's guts. Shit! I hated Bruce too. He was arrogant, abusive mentally and physically and he didn't care about anyone but himself. So in my mind, I say Bruce got what he deserved. Too bad, we'd been dragged into this nonsense. On the other hand, I feel sorry for Mrs. Daisy and Sonya. They didn't deserve to be murdered. All Sonya wanted was for her mother to be loved and appreciated. And since Bruce wasn't doing any of that, Sonya felt it was necessary for her to intervene. Hell, I would've done it too. Maybe not the way Sonya did it. But which, ever way I would've approached it; I would've come out on the winning side.

While I think back, there were a few times I went by Ms. Daisy's house to check on her, but Bruce had already killed her and Sonya and hid their bodies in a freaking storage unit. Damn! I wished I would've known. Who knows, I probably could've saved both of their lives. I know, Dylan is hurting right now. To know that his mother and his sister are gone, Dylan is probably blaming himself for it. I know his heart is heavy right now, and the fact that these cops keep badgering us isn't making his situation any better.

I looked at my wristwatch at least a dozen times but it seemed like the time was standing still. All I wanted to do was get out of there. I had nothing to say to these cops and they knew it. So why string me along when they knew they had nothing on us? I've always been told that most cops abused their authority, which is the main reason why civilians like Dylan and I buck on the system. NWA said it perfectly when they said, "Fuck the police!"

After sitting in this cold ass room, someone finally decides to come in and check on me. Once the door opened fully, the person standing on the other side of it peeps their head around it and my face lit up like a Christmas tree. "Baby, what are you doing in here?" I said with excitement after I stood up.

Dylan walked towards me and then he embraced me. "They said I could come in here and talk to you." He replied after he kissed me a couple of times on my face and lips.

"You know what they are trying to do right?" I whispered into his ear.

"Come on now, you know me better than that. You know, I'm on to them. They wouldn't put us together if they didn't think we would talk about Bruce and your pops." He whispered back.

"Did they tell you how much longer they were going to hold us down here?" I wanted to know.

"Nah, they haven't said anything about that. "If it were up to them, they'd probably try to keep us here all night."

"But that's illegal and they know we know it."

"You're absolutely right. So, that's why I'm letting you to go." Detective Grimes interjected immediately after he walked around the door.

Dylan and I turned around to face him. He had the usual stupid looking grin on his face. The sight of him made me cringe. "So, we can leave right now?" I blurted out.

"Since we didn't find any gun power residue on your boyfriend's hands, I've decided to let you two go." Detective Grimes explained.

Without saying another word, I grabbed Dylan's hand and hauled ass out of that interview. As soon as we crossed the threshold of the doorway, Detective Grimes turned around and said, "Want me to get one of the officers to take you two home?"

"Nah, we're good." Dylan said as we continued heading towards the exit door.

The moment we stepped foot on the earth's soil, I felt a weight lifted from my entire body. "How are we going to get home?" I asked Dylan while we both looked up and down the boulevard.

"We're gonna flag down the next cab we see." Dylan replied.

"Why don't we call Nick?" I suggested.

"Nah, I don't want him coming anywhere near here. I know those bastards are watching our every move so we gotta' keep him under the radar." Dylan told me.

"Do you think they are watching us now?" I kept the conversation going.

"Of course I do." Dylan continued as we started walking down 2nd Avenue. Dylan walks fast so it was hard for me to keep up. "Can you slow down a bit?" I begged.

"You know I'm trying to get away from that police station as fast as I can."

"Did you do it?" I asked him. I wanted to ask him that question immediately after I heard him washing his hands in the bathroom back at our apartment. But now, I finally had a chance to do it.

"Do what?" He asked me while he continued to walk at a fast pace.

"Kill Bruce." I uttered quickly like someone other than Dylan could possibly hear me.

Dylan stopped in his tracks and turned towards me. "Fuck nah! I didn't kill that motherfucker! I wish I had though." Dylan roared.

"So why did you rush into the bathroom to wash your hands before we left the apartment?"

"Because that's what you do after you use the fucking bathroom." He huffed. I could tell he was getting really irritated by my questions.

"Dylan you don't have to talk to me like that." I pointed out.

"Well, how else am I supposed to talk to you? You just asked me if I killed Bruce and when I told you I didn't, you turn around and asked me why was I washing my hands in the fucking bathroom like you didn't believe my first answer."

"It wasn't that I didn't believe you, I just wanted to make sure we were on the same page."

"That shit you just said, doesn't even make sense." He spat and then he stormed off.

I stormed off behind him. "Remember we're on the same team." I yelled.

"Well, act like it." He replied, keeping at least four feet between us.

I didn't say another word to Dylan. I knew he was beginning to mourn his mother and his sister so I left well enough alone.

Finally after walking down a couple of blocks, we were able to flag down a taxi-cab and hop inside of it.

I told the driver where to go and he got us there within ten minutes. After Dylan paid him, we got out of the car and instead of going through the front entrance of our apartment building we took the garage entrance and took the elevator to our floor. The moment Dylan and I exited the elevator, I turned and headed towards our apartment while Dylan went in the opposite direction. "Where are you going?" I asked him.

"I'm going to my mother's house." He replied.

"You know the cops are all over that place so they're not gonna let you go anywhere near the front door."

"Well, then I'll go through the back door." He continued as he made his way towards his car.

I knew I couldn't let him go by himself, no matter how he talked to me when we were leaving the police station. What mattered at this moment was that I needed to be by his side and that's what I am going to do. "Wait, I'm coming too." I said and then I walked towards him.

By the time I got to the trunk of the car, he was already in the driver seat with the engine running. So, the minute after I sat down in the passenger seat he backed out of his assigned parking space and headed back out of the garage.

Dylan was quiet the entire drive to his mother's house. I wanted to ask him how he was feeling but I didn't want him feeling vulnerable if he decided to answer me, so I remained mum. That didn't stop me from keeping a close watch on him from the corner of my eye. He tried to keep a straight face but I knew he was harboring a boatload of pain inside of him. His mother meant the world to him. He loved his sister too. So, not being able to see them anymore or spend time with them is going to be very hard for Dylan to do. Through it all, I only hope that he finds peace and is able to live his life without hate and turmoil. I guess, time will tell.

Mixed Feelings

DYLAN

I love Kira to death, especially because of what she did to her father just so that I could get out of jail and the manslaughter charges could be dropped against me. That took a lot of heart and she sacrificed it. One part of me wanted to grab her and hold her tight and tell her how much I loved her and how much I appreciated her. But dealing with the emotions I am experiencing because of the loss of my mother and sister I can't separate the two feelings. Hopefully I'll figure it out.

When I tried to make a left turn onto my mother's street, I could see that there were police cars blocking both entryways. I drove up to the officer in uniform and asked if he could let me by. "Do you live on this street because I'm only authorized to let homeowners through?" The officer said.

"Yeah, I live at 3920. It's the grey house on the right side of the street." I lied. I was willing to say anything to get this guy to let me by.

"I'm sorry but that's the house the forensics team are scouring so I can't let you by." The officer said.

"Then what am I supposed to do?"

"You're gonna have to wait until the homicide detective who's on this case gives you a call."

"And who is that?"

"The detective heading this investigation is Brady. Give him a call and he will be able to tell you everything you need to know." The officer continued.

"Man fuck you!" I barked and then I turned my car around and sped off in the direction I came from.

As I drove away, anger and rage began to consume me and the next thing I know, I start punching the steering wheel of the car. "Why does these fucking cops keep taking me through unnecessary bullshit? All I want to do is see my mama and my sister. Is that too much to ask?" I roared.

While I spat about everything that was going on wrong around me, Kira started rubbing my back. It was obvious that I was on the verge of having a major breakdown. "Baby,

Detective Grimes told us that your mama and sister's body was found at a storage unit not at the house." She said trying to shine a little light on this unfortunate situation.

"Which storage unit did he say there were at?" I asked her.

"He didn't say. But I'm sure it has to be somewhere near your mother's house. I mean, I can't see Bruce driving that far to get rid of their bodies." She noted.

"Well, google all the storage places in this area and let's hope that one of them is the spot where their bodies are." I instructed her.

Kira googled all the storage space businesses in the area and six of them popped up on her phone. One of them was called Budget Rental Spaces, which was only a mile from where we were. Then there was another storage business called Storages Unlimited and that was a mile and a half away from the first storage place. So, I told Kira that we were going to check that place first and she agreed.

The second after I headed into the direction of the first storage facility, my heart started racing. The fear of seeing my family's bodies lying dead inside of a black bag on top of a gurney gave me an uneasy feeling. I was still trying to come to grips that they were dead, so to see their bodies as evidence made me sick on the stomach. I never pictured my life to be this way. But now that it is, I need to find a way to deal with it.

The drive to the second storage spot only took us three minutes to get there. But I knew instantly that this wasn't the place where my mother and sister's bodies had been found because for one the place was dark and two, it looked abandoned. "This place looks like its been out of business for a while." Kira pointed out.

"Yeah, it does. So, I guess we head to the next spot." I said and then I turned my car back around and sped off.

During the drive to the second storage place my cell phone started ringing. I looked down at the caller ID and noticed it was Nick calling me. I pressed down on the blue tooth function key to connect to my satellite system and then I said, "Hello."

"Dylan, what's up man? I just saw the news. Is it true?" Nick asked me with uncertainty.

I froze for a second before I answered him. I guess the shock factor of someone else knowing that my family was dead, brought me closer to reality. I honestly didn't know how to answer Nick's question. Thankfully Kira stepped in to help me.

"Yes Nick, it's true." Kira said.

"Fuck no! I can't bring myself to believe that." Nick replied.

"Nick, we don't wanna do it either, but we don't have a choice." Kira added.

"Kira put Dylan back on the phone."

"Nick we got you on speaker phone. He can hear you." She said and then she looked over at me. My facial expression hadn't changed one bit while I kept my eyes on the road in front of me.

"Dylan man, what do you need me to do? Just say the word and I'll do it." Nick said.

"He knows that Nick. But right now, it's just a lot of stuff going on so he's gonna need a little bit of time to sort things out."

"Did Bruce really hide their bodies at the storage place on River Drive?" Nick's questions continued.

"How do you know which storage place it was?" I finally spoke.

"Because I just saw it on Channel 12 news station. The woman reporter said that the unit manager called the cops because another unit customer complained about the foul smell coming from it."

"We're on our way there now." I interjected.

"Do you want me to come?" Nick asked me.

"Nah, I'm good. Just stay by the phone and I'll call you back." I said and then Kira disconnected the call.

Within seconds I started driving in the direction of River Drive. "Slow down baby," Kira instructed me in a passive aggressive manner because she knew I was anxious to get to the destination.

Knowing that Kira and I were about to embark on an unfamiliar territory, dealing with the deaths of my mother and my sister, I had to remind myself that it wasn't going to be an easy task. First it was Kira's father, and now it's my mom and Sonya. How much worse could this situation get?

I finally got us to the right place. And when we arrived we noticed that we had entered into a media storm. Four different news stations were on site reporting the traumatic murders of my family. From where we were parked, Kira and I could see the yellow tape covering the entire metal door that I assumed was where my mother and Sonya's bodies were stored. We could also see the gate protecting the storage units were locked. Kira and I sat in the car and watch this media circus in disbelief. We couldn't hear what the reporters were saying, which was good because I really didn't want to fall into a deeper state of depression than I already was.

We sat in the car for at least fifteen long minutes. Kira was ready to leave but I could've stayed here all night. "Baby, how much longer you wanna stay out here?" she asked me.

"I don't know." I told her. But the truth is, I felt that if I left, then I'd be leaving my family here all alone. I mean, that's what happened when I was arrested. They were out here all by themselves. If I weren't in jail behind Kira's father, Bruce wouldn't have gotten a chance to put his fucking hands on them. So, now I blame myself, which is why I don't want to leave here. If I do, then I'll feel like I failed them all over again.

"What do you mean you don't know?"

"I just don't know." I replied sarcastically.

"So, you're saying that we could be out here for another hour or so?"

"I don't know."

"Stop saying, you don't know and fucking talk to me." She spat. I could tell that she was losing patience with me. But at this point, I didn't care. Nothing she could say was going to alter my decision to do anything. And while she waited for me to respond, I didn't part my lips. I heard her take a deep breath breathe and then she exhaled. I figured this was her way of finding a different approach with me.

"Dylan, what's going on in your head?" she asked calmly.

I didn't reply so she pressed the issue.

"Baby, we can't stay out here all night. We've gotta' get a plan in motion." She continued, in a mild tone.

"What kind of plan, Kira? My fucking family is dead! There's no plan in this world that would bring them back." I roared. Tears started forming in my eyes and that's when I knew that this unfortunate situation was breaking me down.

Kira reached over to massage my thigh but I pushed her hand back. "Nah, I ain't feeling that right now." I said in a dismissive manner and I could tell that Kira was in shock because I'd never treated her like this before, so I knew she was hurt. To be perfectly honest, I never lost my mother or sister before either. So it was hard for me to channel my anger and frustrations. “If you would've told me that Bruce was putting his hands on my mama when you first found out, this shit probably would've never happened.” I continued.

“So, you’re blaming those murders on me?” She snapped. She went back into defensive mode quickly.

“You damn right. If you would’ve told me what was going on I would’ve had my mama moved out of her house and I would’ve had Bruce dealt with. But nah, you kept that shit to yourself like you do everything else. You got so many fucking secrets, I don’t know who the fuck you are anymore. And I’m starting not to trust you either.”

“Are you fucking kidding me right now?” She yelled.

“Whatcha’ think I’m playing?” I stood my ground. I wasn’t feeling anything she was saying. My family was dead and this whole thing could’ve been avoided if she had just told me.

“I can’t believe you’re talking to me like this.”

“Well, believe it!”

“You know what? Fuck you! Take me home!”

I didn't say another word to Kira. I was angry and hurt. She was angry and upset, so the best thing I could do for her was take her home. I mean, it wasn't like she could do anything to make things better. She fucked that up when she kept that secret from me. Not to mention, her father was the cause of me going to fucking jail in the first place. If that motherfucker would've stayed in his lane and minded his business while he was a guest in my apartment, then he wouldn't be dead, I wouldn't have gone to jail and my mama and sister would still be alive.

Kira and I sat there in silence and I thought about what she said and that's when I turned my car around and sped off in the direction of our apartment. I figured that if she had stayed out here with me, all we'd do was argue and I don't need that drama, especially since I'm trying to deal with the lost of my family. So if separating us is the key to giving me a clear head and a peace of mind to think about what's going to be best for me, then that's what I want. Because if I do the opposite then I may end up doing something really stupid that would put me back in jail and who knows, my stint could possibly be longer the last time.

Playing the Blame Game

KIRA

My mind was spinning in circles while I tried to digest the level of disrespect I had just gotten from Dylan. At one point I wanted to punch him in his fucking face. I was hurting pretty badly once he told me how he really felt about this whole thing. Does he not realize that I loved his family just as much as he did? If I had known that Bruce was going to kill them, Nick and I would've done everything within our power to prevent it. Better yet, we would've probably ended Bruce's life ourselves. But Bruce always made it difficult for us to get to him. If he wasn't hiding behind the curtains in the bedroom window, he was hiding behind the front door. Not only that, he had the police on his side. We could never win. I hope one day Dylan sees that. If not, I don't know where I relationship will end up. Will see.

After he dropped me back off to our apartment building. I was too tired to enter the building through the garage area so I got him to drop me off in front near the valet area. At this point, I could care less who saw me and who was whispering when I walked back them. Dealing with Dylan's accusations stung me really hard and I needed to find a way to deal with it.

Our usual doorman opened the glass door to the lobby and let me in. He smiled and spoke to me. I didn't have the energy to open my mouth to speak, but I did give him a half smile as I walked by him. When I entered the building and walked through the lobby, it was shocking to see that no one was around. I didn't even see the concierge director standing behind his desk. This was weird because throughout the time I've lived here, someone was always at that post. Well, since I don't own the building, it's not my problem.

I headed towards the elevators and bumped into an elderly white couple that I've only seen a few times in passing. I didn't know their name and I'm sure they did know mine but to prevent from being rude I said hello. The man spoke back but his wife looked at me from head to toe and then she rolled her eyes. I couldn’t tell you if she's racist or just down right rude, but I will say that she picked the wrong day to have an attitude with me. And I made sure that she knew it. “Why couldn't you just speak to me like your husband did? Are you insecure because I could have an affair with your husband and spend all of his money?” I hissed. I even went below the belt and said, “My pussy is really really wet and from the looks of him, he’d enjoy every inch of it.”

“You are nothing but a whore!” She snapped. Her face became red instantly.

“Lady, I'll be anything you want me to be.” I commented and smiled.

Before the woman could utter another word the elevator door opened and her husband grabbed her by the arm and pulled her onto the elevator. I started to get on the elevator with them so I could create more drama with the old lady, but I decided against it. I didn't want her to have a heart attack because Detective Grimes would make it his business to find a way to charge me with it.

I jumped on the next elevator when the door opened and took it straight to my floor. Thankfully, I didn’t run into any of my neighbors. I wasn't in the mood to do any more explaining about my constant run-ins with the police. And besides, they didn't need to be in my business anyway.

After I walked into my apartment I grabbed my cell phone from my purse and then I sat my purse down on the coffee table right before I sat down on the sofa. I searched for Nick's cell phone number in my call log and when I found it, I pressed the send button. His cell phone rang three times before he answered it. The sound of his voice gave me a sense of relief. "Hey Kira, what's up?" Nick said.

"Listen, Dylan just dropped me back off at the apartment and then he left. I don't know where he's going or what he's about to do but I need you to call him ASAP."

"How long has he been gone?"

"Five minutes."

"He might be coming over my house." Nick suggested.

"I really don't care, especially after the way he talked to me. But I do need you to talk some sense into him because if he comes back home tonight with that bullshit stunt he pulled after we got off the phone with you, then I'm out of here. He can kiss me goodbye."

"What did he say?"

"Nick, he cursed me out like I was some bimbo in the streets. Talking about it's my fault that his mama and sister got killed because if I would've told him about it he would've taken her out of the house before Bruce got a chance to do anything to her."

"Wow! That's not cool to blame you. But I'm gonna talk to him though." Nick assured me.

"Well, I hope he listens to you because if he doesn't and comes back home with that bullshit, I'm packing up and I'm gonna leave him for good."

"Kira, don't jump to conclusions. He's hurt and this is his way of venting."

"I don't know Nick. I've never seen him act this way and especially towards me. I think what sent him over the edge was when the cops came here earlier and escorted both of us down to the police station to ask us questions about Bruce."

"The cops came by your crib again?"

"Yes, they did. And I was livid too. Detective Grimes and that other detective came to our front door asking where Dylan was because they wanted to tell him that they found Mrs. Daisy and Sonya dead. But then when they started talking about how they found Bruce's dead, they said that it appeared to be a suicide but they wanted to make sure, so they came there to escort us to the police station so they could check our hands for gun powder residue and ask us a few questions."

"Those cops are fucking assholes. They know that Bruce killed himself. Shit! Even the fucking reporters know it. They came by your place so they could harass y'all." Nick said.

"We know."

"Y'all might have to move across town or go on vacation for a while because if you don't, they're gonna find different ways to fuck with you."

"I'm not doing anything with him until I get an apology."

"Don't worry about that. He loves you Kira so I know he's going to do that. Especially after he calms down and realizes what happened between y'all."

I became silent for a moment and then I let out a long sigh. "I wish I would've kicked in Mrs. Daisy's front door and took her out of that house."

"Kira, you can't sit around there and put all the blame on yourself."

"Dylan said it first."

"Well, forget that he said it. When I see him I'm gonna talk to him so don't you worry."

"A'ight. Text me later after you talk to him."

"You got it." Nick said and then we ended our call.

Immediately after I got off the phone with Nick I laid my head back on one of the sofa pillows and thought about the conversation I had just had with him. He was right I can't blame myself for what happened to his family. I did everything within my power to get to see Mrs. Daisy. So I hope when Dylan returns he'll have a better outlook about what happened and apologizes to me for the way he talked to me before he dropped me off. But you know what? Even if he doesn't apologize, I'll still forgive him. I mean, if I loss two loved ones at the same time, I'd be upset and hurt too.

While I was thinking about ways to help Dylan cope with his loss ones, I was also thinking about my father. I didn't really want to kill my father. I looked up to him as a child growing up. He was the best male figure I could ever have. But then over the years, his ways changed. Don't get me wrong he was a loving man, but when he started trying to run my life our relationship began to suffer. One thing led to the next and then our conversations started happening few and far between. The next thing I know, I only called him when I felt like it was time to check on him. I wish I could turn back the hands of time. I swear, I would do everything right. Wishful thinking though, because it would never happen.

I looked at my phone a couple of times trying to decide if I should call Dylan or not. But then I figured it would be best to give him some time and space, he'll come around. And in the meantime, I'll just stay out of his way.

My mind shifted from thinking about Dylan to thinking about Bruce killing Mrs. Daisy and Sonya. I now realize that none of the cops told us how Bruce killed them, which I thought was mind-boggling. I guess they were so fixated on getting Dylan and I to confess to the murders, they forgot all about giving us the details. It's okay though, because I'm sure that I'm going to see them again. Maybe, sooner than later.

According to my wristwatch, I've been lying here for a little over one hour and I can't seem to relax and clear my head for nothing in the world. I reached for my cell phone to see if Nick or Dylan had text me, but when I looked at it closely I noticed that I hadn't received a phone call or text from either of them. But I was sure that I would hear from them soon.

Dylan Is All I Have

KIRA

Who said life would be easy? I hadn't realized that I had fallen asleep until my cell phone started ringing. I looked at the time on my cell phone and noticed that it was a little after midnight. I also noticed that Nick was calling me. I answered the call on the third ring. "Hello," I said.

"Hey Kira, is Dylan with you?"

"No he's not."

"Did he ever come back home?"

"I haven't seen him since he dropped me off? Wait, are you saying that he never came to your house?"

"Yeah, he never stopped by." Nick assured me. And that's when a ball of emotions exploded inside of me. I was still angry with him from the way he talked to me earlier but I put all that to the side because I felt like something bad had happened to him.

Instantly a lump formed in my throat, the hairs on my arms stood up and then it felt like my heart collapsed into the pit of my stomach. I was having an array a feelings engulf me at the same time. I couldn't tell you if I was coming or going. But I knew that if I couldn't control my emotions, surely I was going to have a nervous breakdown.

"Kira, are you there?" Nick asked. But I couldn't open my mouth to respond.

"Kira, can you hear me?" His questions continued.

"Kira, if you can hear me please say something. You're scaring me right now." Nick expressed. I could tell that he was getting nervous so I forced my way to respond. "I can hear you. I'm here." I managed to say.

"Yo' baby girl, you were scaring the hell out of me. Please don't do that again."

"I'm sorry," I told him, even though I didn't do it purposely. I was literally plagued with a gamut of feelings that I couldn't express, so how in the hell was I able to talk? I couldn't. So that's the bottom line.

"Listen, we've got to find out where Dylan is, because this is not like him. I've never known him to go on a road trip without telling either one of us where he's going."

"I know." I agreed.

"Well, I tell you what, I'm going to ride out to a couple of spots and see if he's there. And if I find him, I'll call you immediately."

"So you just want me to stay at home and wait for you to call me?"

"Come on now Kira, you know Dylan would go crazy if I had you out this time of the night."

"But it's for a perfectly good reason." I replied, trying to make a point.

"Look, I'm sorry, but I can't do it." Nick said with finality and then he said, "Keep your phone close because I'll be calling you within the hour."

I let out a sigh. "Yeah, whatever." I said and then I ended the call.

As I sat there on the sofa, I thought to myself that I couldn't sit in this apartment and wait for Nick to find Dylan. Was he crazy to think I would listen to him? I may look nice, sweet and delicate, but I'm a bitch from the streets and I can handle myself, which is why I'm getting ready to hop in my car and go on the hunt for my man too.

I got up from the sofa, used the bathroom, washed my hands and face with a face towel and then I slipped on a pair of Yeezy's, grabbed my purse and my car keys and headed out the door.

It didn't take me long to get in my car and make my way out of the parking garage. I had no idea where I was going, so I started off going to nearby sports bars. I drove by the Sandbar first and when I didn't see his car parked outside, I kept driving. The next spot I drove by was the Sports Grill, but once again I couldn't locate his car so I moved along. The third spot I drove by was called Duffy's and when I didn't see his car parked along the street I kept driving.

I can't lie, there were over a dozen sports bars and nightclubs on each block running down the main street of Miami. And the people that patronize these businesses were everywhere you turn your head. I knew that looking for Dylan on this busy strip would be a task, but I also knew that I couldn't go home without him. I wouldn't be able to sit in my apartment in peace if I didn't. Dylan meant the world to me and I was going to show him just how much.

The Miami night air was so beautiful and breezy but that wasn't helping me find my man. I swear I wanted to give up and go back home, but my loyalty to him convinced me to stay out here and beat the pavement if I had to. But at the same time, I'm gonna have to think long and hard about where he could be. This city isn't but so big. I mean, come on give me a break here. I need some answers.

Meanwhile I wrecked my brain trying to figure out where Dylan could be, that's when it dawned on me to ride by his sister's or mother's house. "He's gotta be there." I mumbled to myself. And as I was preparing to make a right turn at the next block, a car pulled up on the left side of my car. I couldn't see who it was so I turned around to get a look, and I was met with the death look of Kendrick. I did a double take just to make sure that my eyes weren't playing tricks on me. To my dismay, my eyes weren't deceiving me. It was Kendrick in the flesh. I waited for him to say something but he didn't. He just looked at me while his car drove by. He turned his head forward as his car rode past mine. Luckily, I was making a right turn at this corner, because if I wasn't who knows what Kendrick would've said or done to me.

I couldn't get away from this strip quick enough after seeing Kendrick roll by me. I mean, was it a coincidence or what? Was he following me? And if so, how long had he been doing it? How the fuck did he know where I was? This shit with him is getting creepier by the moment, so I wanna tell Dylan about it. But was it a good idea? I guess I will find out.

Mrs. Daisy's house was going to be my first stop. I figured that if Dylan was anywhere, it would be there since there wasn't a sighting of him hanging out on the strip. Thankfully the traffic wasn't bad on my way there. Traffic in Miami can be a little tedious at times, but tonight, things were different and I welcomed it.

I believed my drive to Mrs. Daisy's house was going to be easy. But as soon as I turned onto her block, my anxiety started mounting. Images of Bruce's dead body wouldn't leave my mind. I'm sure it was a gory scene with blood and fragments of his brain were splattered everywhere. Who goes and commits suicide? You've got to be a very sick individual to put a gun to your head and pull the trigger. I mean, if he was that depressed, why didn't he just leave? He didn't have to kill

Sonia and Mrs. Daisy. They didn't deserve the cards he dealt to them. In my mind he was a troubled, selfish man so I hope he gets what he deserves in the afterlife.

While I was in deep thought, I cruised onto the block where Mrs. Daisy's home was and I instantly recognized Dylan's car parked in front of her house. Seeing this, my heart skipped a beat. I was both anxious and relieved at the same time. I exhaled to try and calm my nerves as I approached my man's car.

Immediately after I parked my car behind Dylan's, I left the engine running while I exited my car. And without hesitation, I scrambled to the driver side of his car and when I peered through his tinted window, I realized that he wasn't inside so I stood up and looked at the house and that's when I saw Dylan lying down on the porch. "Baby, what are you doing?" I yelled and then I took off and started running towards him.

He didn't respond so I called his name again. "Dylan," I yelled as I moved towards him.

Instead of answering me, he moved his body a little while he laid in a fetal position. The moment I walked up the steps and got within 2ft. of him, I looked at him closely, noticing that his eyes were slightly opened. So, I kneeled down and placed both of my hands on each side of his face and lifted it up enough to where I could sit next to him and lay his head on my lap. "Kira, is that you?" He said, his words were slurred and that's when I knew that he had been drinking. I cradled his head and then I leaned my head forward and gave him a kiss on his forehead.

"Baby, you've been drinking." I said.

"I only had a little bit." He replied.

"What are you doing here?" I asked him while I continued to cradle his head in my arms.

"I was just waiting out here for my mama to come home." He said. I learned quickly that Dylan was in denial that his mother was dead.

"Baby, I'm sorry but she's not coming home." I said with caution.

"But she is," he began to say, "Just wait and see." He continued. I could see that he was really adamant about seeing his mother again.

At this point, I saw no way to convince him that Mrs. Daisy wasn't coming home. It was clear that he was severely intoxicated and nothing I could say was going to make him think otherwise.

"Guess what else, baby?" He started speaking again.

"What is it?" I replied, preparing myself for Dylan to say something else outlandish.

"Sonya is coming over here too. She called my cell phone and left a message telling me that her and my mama were together and that they're gonna be here in a minute." He said and gave me a half smile. If I hadn't known what was really going on, I would've believed that Dylan was telling the truth. But since I knew the real story, I couldn't allow myself to get caught up in this fantasy world he was creating.

"Baby, it's really late so let's get out of here." I suggested.

"Nah, I can't leave until they come. They told me that they were on their way." Dylan protested.

"Okay listen, I'll tell you what. Let's get in the car and go home and as soon as we wake up in the morning we can come back over here." I said, trying to compromise.

"No Kira, I can't leave. They'll be here in a minute."

Frustrated by Dylan's cooperation, I got up the gumption to tell him the truth. I lifted him up from my lap and sat him up enough where we were face to face. I wasn't sure how he was going to take this information I was about to give him, but at this point I couldn't worry about it. So I looked at him and said, "Dylan, Sonya and your mama aren't coming here. They are dead baby. Bruce killed them."

Dylan's facial expression changed. He went from happy to sad and confused in a matter of seconds. "You don't know what you're talking about. Bruce hasn't done shit to my family. I'll kill him if he ever touches them!" Dylan hissed. It was truly scary to see how delusional Dylan had become after hearing what Bruce had done to his loved ones. But I refused to let him wallow in this level of depression.

"Come on, let's get out of here." I said after I stood to my feet.

"I'm not leaving here until they get here first." He challenged me.

I grabbed his arm and pulled him up on his feet. He stumbled a bit, so I grabbed him by the other arm to prevent him from falling. "Get off me Kira," He said, trying to resist me.

"I'm not letting you go, so come on." I told him.

"No! I told you I wasn't going!" Dylan spat and then he snatched both of his arms from me. The weight of his body was too much for me so I stumbled backwards. Dylan had stumbled backwards in the opposite directions, but neither one of us fell.

Refusing to back down I walked towards Dylan again and grabbed him. This time I grabbed him by the jacket he was wearing. I wrapped my hand around the bottom of his jacket, where the elastic was and tugged on him. "Come on Dylan we have to go. It's late." I said, trying to reason with him.

"I'm not leaving until I see my mama and my sister." He replied while he stood his ground.

"Baby, they are not coming back. They are dead!" I blurted out with frustration. I was at my wits end with Dylan being in denial.

Before I could blink my eyes, Dylan swung at me with an open hand, slapping the taste out of my mouth. Taken aback, I jumped back a couple of feet and placed my hand across the cheek that Dylan had just hit. Shocked by his actions, I stood there trying to figure out why he had just hit me. At first, he disrespected me verbally and now he takes it upon himself to hit me. What is it going to be next? Is he going to start physically abusing me? If that's the case, I want no parts of it.

Instead of arguing with him and trying to get him to apologize for what he had just done,

I turned around I walked away. "Where are you going?" He yelled while I was walking towards my car.

"Fuck you!" I yelled back.

"So is like that?" He yelled again. But I ignored him. I wasn't about to have a full-fledged yelling match with him. Since he wants to sit outside his mother's house waiting for her to return, then so be it. I will not have any parts of it.

When I got back into my car I looked in the direction where Dylan was standing and noticed that he had already turned around and went back to sit down on the porch. I shook my head with sheer disappointment. I can't tell you how long he's going to sit there but I can say that I am burnt out with his antics so I'm going to let his friend Nick handle it.

While I was buckling my seatbelt, I used my Bluetooth system to call Nick. "Kira, I was about to call you," he said immediately after he answered my call.

"Well, if you're calling me to tell me you can't find Dylan, don't bother because he and I both are sitting outside of his mother's house." I told him.

"What are y'all doing there?" He asked.

"When I didn't hear back from you, I decided to take a ride over here to his mother's house and as soon as I pulled up, I look out my passenger side window and see him lying down on the porch." I explained.

"Is he right there with you now?"

"No, he's sitting down on the porch."

"Okay now I'm confused. Why is he sitting on the porch?"

"Well, first of all he's drunk. He's so drunk that he believes his mom and sister are going to pull up to this house any minute now."

"Oh wow! Are you serious?"

"Yes I am serious. But that's not it," I said and then I fell silent, "when I tried to convince him otherwise, he gets all upset and starts yelling at me. And then when I got fed up, I grabbed him and tried to escort him to my car so we can go home, but then he slaps me."

"He did what?"

"You heard me. Your best friend put his hands on me. He smacked me on my face. And after he did it, he stood there like a fucking clown. So I walked away from him before I said something that I'd probably regret later."

"Did he apologize?"

"Hell no! He didn't apologize. And that's one of the reasons I got in my car. Now if you don't come and get him, then he's gonna be out here all night long waiting for Mrs. Daisy and Sonya to come back to that house."

"Ahh man, he's not dealing with this well, huh?"

"I can't tell you how he's dealing with it. But I do know that he's in denial. And there's nothing you or I can say to him that's going to make him believe anything different. He's gonna have to see it on his own."

"That's so unfortunate. But I'll tell you what, I'll be there in about 10 minutes."

I sighed heavily and then I said, "All right. I'll be here."

An Ace In the Hole

KIRA

As bad as I wanted to curse Dylan out for slapping me across my damn face, I held my composure and got his friend Nick to step in and help out with this situation. Now if Nick hadn't agreed to come, Dylan would've been up shits creek without a paddle.

I saw Nick's SUV approaching my car through my rearview mirror. After he parked his truck behind my car, he got out and closed the driver side door and I stepped out of my car to greet him. We met at the trunk of my car. "Do you see him sitting over there on the porch?" I asked.

"Yeah, I see him." Nick replied and then he stepped away from me and started walking towards the front porch.

I crossed my arms and stood quietly next to my car and waited to see how Nick was going to handle Dylan's intoxicated behavior.

"Dylan, what's going on man?" I heard Nick say.

"Whatcha' talking about?" I heard Dylan reply.

"Why are you so drunk? Got something you want to talk about?" Nick wanted to know.

"I'm not drunk. I only had a few drinks." Dylan said.

"Nah man, you look like you had more than two."

"Come on now, Nick I ain't hurting nobody. I'm just chilling here waiting for my mama and my sister to come home."

"Dylan, they aren't coming home, man."

"Yes, they are. My sister left me a message on my phone. Wanna hear it?" Dylan argued as he looked for his cell phone that was in his front pocket. After he grabbed it, he pulled it out and tried to hand it to Nick..

"You ain't gotta' do that. I believe you." Nick said and then he pushed Dylan's hand back.

"I know damn well you do! I don't lie about nothing." Dylan spat.

I saw Nick turn his attention towards me for a second and then he turned his attention back towards Dylan. "Dylan, let me use your phone for a minute so I can call your sister."

Dylan reached back into his pocket, grabbed his cell phone and then he handed it to Nick. I watched Nick as he pretended to make a call. "Hey Sonya, I'm glad you answered the phone," he started off saying, "Me and Dylan are here sitting on the porch at your mama's house waiting for y'all to get here. So can you tell me what time you're coming?" Nick continued and then he paused for a brief second.

While I was watching Nick pretend to be talking to someone, I couldn't help but to see how attentive Dylan had become as he watched Nick.

"So, you're not coming until tomorrow?" Nick said loud enough for Dylan and I both could hear. "Okay, thanks for letting me know because Dylan was gonna wait until you guys got here." He concluded and then he acted like he disconnected the call. "Your sister said that her and your mama were really tired so they weren't coming here until tomorrow morning." Nick lied.

Dylan sat there with a look of confusion. For a moment, I was beginning to feel sorry for him. He sat there like a lost puppy. He acted like he wanted to believe Nick, but then he looked like he was having some doubts. I wanted to intervene so badly, but I decided against it. I felt like Nick didn't need my help. He was doing a great job without me.

"Come on man, let's get out of here." Nick said as he extended his hand for Dylan to grab it.

Dylan was hesitant at first, but Nick wore him down. "Don't worry. I'll be glad to bring you back over here as soon as the sun comes up." Nick promised.

Finally Dylan, let his guard down and allowed Nick to escort him away from the house. Nick looked at me and said, "Do you want me to carry him to my house?"

"Yes please. Maybe in the morning you will be able to talk to him and see where his mind is because I've had enough for one day." I expressed.

"A'ight, well keep your phone on and I'll get with you a morning. Who knows, maybe he'll be back to himself after he gets him some rest."

"I hope so." I said nonchalantly and then I got back into my car.

I left before Nick had a chance to buckle Dylan into his seatbelt. I needed to get away from them and fast. I had a lot going on in my head and I needed to find a way to release it before it consumed me.

The drive back to my apartment gave me a chance to think about all the drama I had going on in my life. I had a long laundry list of shit too, but the last event that had just transpired was enough for me to take a back seat and try to re-evaluate my life to see what's important and what's not.

To have Dylan go out and get drunk, curse me out and then put his hands on me, was the final straw. There's no doubt in my mind that he is going to come home in the morning and apologize for how he treated me tonight. I just hope that Nick is able to get in his head and convince him that not only has he lost his family but he can't allow himself to go out and get drunk and act like he did any more, because the next time the cops could pull him over and take him to jail. Or he could cause a terrible accident that could kill himself and an innocent victim. That would be a tragedy, which is why I pray that he pulls it together.

Back at my apartment, I took a long hot shower and then I slipped on a set of pjs. I crawled into my bed soon thereafter. While I was in bed, I grabbed the TV remote from my nightstand and powered on the television. I sifted through most of the channels and finally decided to watch an infomercial about a copper-cooking pan. I have to admit that the recipes they were using to cook in this pan looked really tasty, but it wasn't enough to keep me awake. And the next thing I knew, I was in Lala land.

What the Fuck Is Wrong With Me?

DYLAN

I couldn't understand a damn word Nick was saying. I saw his mouth moving while he was driving but I was totally oblivious. I blinked my eyes a few times to get rid of the fuzziness but that didn't seem to work either. While Nick was driving to God knows where, I was blinded a number of times by the nightlights on the streets. The lights became so unbearable that I closed my eyes altogether.

I didn't realize that Nick's truck had stopped until he dragged me into his apartment and laid me down on his sofa. Once again he tried to have a conversation with me but I couldn't make out one word he said. His mouth moved for what seemed like forever. But at the blink of an eye, everything got dark. And then it was quiet.

I heard a man's voice speaking. I thought I was dreaming but when I heard his voice long enough I knew it was Nick. "Why the fuck you keep stressing me out over dumb shit?" He said and then he fell silent for a few seconds. "I already told you where I was. And I ain't gonna say it again." He continued, sounding more aggravated by the second. That's when I opened my eyes and realized that it was light out.. I also realized that I was lying down on a sofa in Nick's apartment while he was arguing with some chick on the phone.

Immediately after I lifted my head from the end of the pillow, I felt a sharp pain ignite around the temple area of my head. I knew then that I had a hangover so I laid my head back down on the pillow and closed my eyes, hoping that this would ease the pain a little. But of course it didn't. Nick arguing with that woman on the phone didn't help my situation either. Damn I wished I were home.

After lying there for a few minutes I called out Nick's name. "Yo' Nick, I need some aspirin?" I said it loud enough for him to hear me, but without me yelling.

I heard Nick walking towards the living room. "Let me call you back." I heard him say.

"Sounds like you gotta headache." He said as he walked by me and headed into the kitchen.

"It feels more like a migraine." I commented while I watched him grab a bottle of aspirin from the cabinet and a bottle of water from the refrigerator.

"That's what happens when you go out drinking." He mentioned as he handed me both bottles of aspirin and water. I opened the bottle of aspirin and poured two tablets into my hand after I sat up on the sofa. "I hope this shit works." I said to Nick and then I placed both pills on my tongue. After I opened the bottle of water and poured a couple of ounces into my mouth, I swallowed it and placed the bottle of water down on the coffee table in front of me. Nick watched me from the Lazy boy recliner as I laid my head back down on the pillow. "I bet you're wondering why you're here, huh?" Nick asked me.

"Is it that obvious?"

"Come on now, we've been friends long enough."

"Well, let's hear it."

"Do you remember anything that happened last night?"

"Yeah, I remember getting pissed off with Kira because she wanted me to leave the storage place where my mom and sister's bodies were. So I ended up dropping her off at home and then I went to one of the local bar spots and got drunk. But I don't remember anything after that."

"So you don't remember driving to your mom's house last night?"

"Nah, I don't."

"Well, I got a call from Kira last night asking me if you were with me? And I told her no so she got worried and wanted to go out looking for you. But I told her that wouldn't be a good idea and that I'd do it. Well, let's just say that she didn't listen to me and left the apartment anyway and did her own search. And when she found you lying down on your mom's front porch she tried to get you to come home with her but you gave her a hard time, protesting to leave. So, after many failed attempts she called me and had me come and pick you up."

"Where is my car?"

"I think it's still parked in front of your mom's house. But what you need to be thinking about right now is how you're going to patch things up with Kira."

"She'll be a'ight. We have arguments all the time and make up the very next day." I told Nick.

"She told me that you hit her in the face."

"I did what?" I wanted him to repeat himself. I hadn't ever put my hands on Kira so to hear that I'd done that to her was a hard pill to swallow.

"She told me that you smacked her across the face when she was trying to walk you to her car so she could take you home."

"Nick please tell me you're bullshitting me."

"I wish I could, man. But it's the truth."

"I wonder what made me do it?" I asked aloud, hoping Nick would have an answer for me.

"I think it's because you had too much alcohol."

"Damn! I'm feeling really fucked up right now. I can't believe I put my hands on her."

"Dylan, you were giving us both a hard time last night."

"I gave you problems too?"

"Yeah, I was trying to put you in my truck and you kept telling me that you weren't leaving because Sonya called and told you that her and your mom was coming back to the house. So you wanted to wait for them."

"I said that?"

"Yep,"

"Damn, I must've been really drunk."

"You had to be because you were saying some crazy shit last night."

"Did I try to hit you?"

"Nah, you didn't try to hit me but you cursed me out though. I'm just glad you're all right now. I mean, because if Kira hadn't found you, you probably would've tried to drive home last night and got into a bad accident."

"Damn! That would've been messed up."

"Yeah, it would've." Nick commented and then he said, "So, what happened when the cops took y'all back down to the police station?"

"Yo' Nick, they were getting on my fucking nerves. First they come to my house to tell me that they found my mom's and my sister's bodies. And then they tell me that they found Bruce's body too and that it looked like a suicide, but they wanted to make sure that it was, so they wanted to take me and Kira down to their office so they could ask us some questions."

"Did they handcuff y'all?"

"Detective Grimes slapped the cuffs on me while they were in my apartment but when they took us downstairs, they didn't make me wear them."

"So what did they say?"

"They said a lot of shit, but I did answer them. I told them to call my attorney and talk to him."

Nick started laughing. "I know that cop was pissed when you said that."

"Yeah, he was. But he got over it."

"So how long did they make y'all stay down there?"

"Well, since I wasn't answering any of their questions, they asked me if they could test my hands for gun powder residue and I said yeah, so when it was done they let me and Kira go."

"So they think you had something to do with Bruce's death?"

"Yeah, they did."

"Yo' Dylan, I'm sorry about what happened to your family. If I could have done anything different, I would. I loved your mother like she was my own. So to hear about what happened to her really breaks my heart. I swear, if the cops didn't come to your mom's crib when me and Kira went over there the other day, I would've killed Bruce myself. He was a fucking coward. And he used to always hide in the house, peeping out the window like a weakling. I swear Dylan, I hate that motherfucker!" Nick expressed. I could tell that he was really hurt behind my family's murders.

"It's all good man. We'll get through this." I assured him. So what's going on with that new spot we got?" I changed the subject. Truthfully speaking, I didn't want to dwell on about what happened to my family. I wanted to get as far away as I possibly could from that conversation.

"The new spot is doing good. I picked up 15 grand from them last night." Nick told me.

"Have the niggas from the Terrace called to re-up?"

"Nah, they haven't. And I was meaning to talk to you about that shit anyway."

"What's up?"

"I think those niggas at that spot are stepping on our shit so they can stretch it out and make more money. But their plan ain't working because now they can't get rid of it."

"What makes you think they're doing that?"

"Because that nigga name Russ told me that one of the dope fiends that normally get their dope from the Terrace came by his spot to score and started complaining, saying that the niggas from Terrace spot dope ain't good anymore."

"I'm telling you right now, that if I find out that those motherfuckers are diluting my dope, there is going to be hell to pay." I told Nick. My blood was boiling on the inside. "I'm so tired of motherfuckers playing games with me. Do they know that I will kill them on the spot? I will cut their fucking heads off, giftwrap them and send them to their baby mamas. I know one thing, they better have a good explanation about why my dope isn't selling like it was before." I continued and then I sat straight up on the sofa.

"Is your head feeling any better?" Nick asked me.

"Yeah, my headache is almost gone." I replied and then I stood up on my feet. I stumbled a bit but I caught my balance.

Nick quickly got up from his seat. "You sure you're right?"

"I'm good. I'm just trying to go to the bathroom." I said and then I walked towards the hallway bathroom. Immediately after I went inside, I started urinating in the toilet and while I was doing that I started thinking about what I was going to do to those motherfuckers that were playing with my money. Every body in Miami knows how crazy I can get when niggas fuck with shit that belongs to me. And now I have to show them again.

I flushed the toilet when I was done pissing. I didn't feel like washing my hands so I walked back out of the bathroom. "Think you can take me to my mom's house so I can pick up my car?" I asked Nick as soon as my eyes landed on him.

He was in the kitchen pouring himself a glass of grape juice when I approached him. "Yeah sure. Let me get this juice and I'll be ready." He told me.

I patted my pants pocket to make sure I had my car keys and when they jingled, I told Nick I would meet him outside at his truck.

On the way to my mother's house Nick and I started talking about how we were going to deal with the guys at the Terrace spot and what time we were going to pay those guys a visit. "How do you want to approach this situation?" Nick asked me.

"I'm not sure. I need to figure it out. Because the way I'm feeling right now with the shit that happened to my mom and my sister, if one of those motherfuckers lie to me or say something slick out of their mouths, I'm killing them on the spot."

"Now don't get me wrong, I'm not going against you, but I do think that we need to be a little careful about how we run up on those niggas because we got too much heat on us right now to be talking about killing somebody."

"I'm witcha'." I told him, but I wasn't in the mood to be told what to do. I knew Nick meant well, but I'm tired of being the nice guy. Being the nice guy allowed Bruce to murder my family so those days are over.

"Did Kira tell you about the sacrifice she made so that you could come home?"

"Yeah she told me."

"Well, then don't get caught slipping because you want to make a point. Because if you do, the sacrifice she made will be in vain. She loves you Dylan, so don't fuck it up."

Instead of responding to what Nick said, I just sat in the passenger seat and started staring at the birds that were flying in the sky. They were free to roam around and do whatever they liked. I want that type of freedom too. But will I have it? I wish I had the answer.

Nick pulled up in front of my mother's house 8 minutes later. I told him I'd call him after I got home, took a shower and got dressed. “Be careful,” he said and then he pulled off.

I tried not to look at my mother’s house before I got into my car but I couldn't help it. It felt like her energy was pulling me in that direction. I got choked up thinking about how I allowed Bruce to come into my father's house and beat my mother. What kind of son am I to allow that to happen? I should've spent more time with her. But now it’s too late. And even though I won't ever be able to punish Bruce for what he did to my family, I promise I will make someone else pay for it.

What's Next On the Agenda?

KIRA

The sun woke me up the following morning. And even though I was asleep for six hours, it didn't feel like it. My body was restless and so was my mind. Dylan had a lot to do with it. But I was determined that I was going to get out of this rut today.

After I crawled out of bed I headed into the kitchen and made myself a hot cup of tea. I carried my tea with me and moseyed my way into the living room and took a seat on the sofa. I took a sip of the tea and then I sat it down on the coffee table in front of me. I grabbed the remote control and powered on the television. "Please don't let me see no news." I mumbled to myself. All I wanted to do was take my mind off everything that has happened, so the last thing I wanted to do was see a journalist on television broadcasting news about my father's murder, Bruce's suicide or Dylan's family. I can honestly say that I had heard enough bad news for the rest of my life.

While I sifted through channels, I purposely skipped over the news channels and settled on watching the game show Family Feud. Steve Harvey was looking dapper as usual. But his comedic ability is what had me glued to the TV. And even though watching this show was a temporary fix, it took my mind off the drama going on in my life with all the jokes he cracked while interacting with the contestants. I even found myself playing along by shouting out the answers to the questions.

Now when they say good things don't last always, believe them, because as soon as I got all into the game, I heard my cell phone ringing from my bedroom. I hopped up from the sofa and ran into my bedroom to get it. I looked at the caller ID and noticed it was Dylan calling me. I answered his call on the third ring. "Hello," I said.

"Hey baby, are you home?" He asked me. I could tell he was trying to fill me out to see if I was in a bad mood.

"Yes, I'm home." I told him.

"Well, Nick dropped me back off to pick up my car, so I'll be home in a few minutes."

I sigh heavily. "Alright I'll be here." I replied and then we ended the call.

Dylan walked into our apartment 20 minutes later. I was lounging on the sofa when our eyes connected. He smiled at me after he closed and locked the front door. But I refused to smile back. Believe me, he felt the tension in the air so he walked over to the sofa and took a seat next to me. I acted like I was watching television, but I had my peripheral vision on full blast. "Let me see your face." He said.

"For what?" I asked sarcastically.

"Nick told me that I slapped you in your face last night." He replied while he grabbed my chin and turned my face around so he could get a good look at me.

"That's enough." I said and I jerked my head back 10 seconds later.

"So, I can't touch you right now?"

"Do you think you deserve to?" I questioned him, giving him an evil facial expression.

"Listen baby, I am so sorry. I love you with all my heart! You're my life and I never wanted to hurt you." Dylan started apologizing.

"Why did you go out drinking last night? I saw a side of you that I've never seen before."

"I know. I know. Trust me baby, it won't ever happen again." He promised.

"Do you remember anything you said to me last night?"

"No, not really."

"So you don't remember telling me that you talked to your sister and she said that she was bringing your mother home last night?"

"I remember saying something like that." He admitted.

"Well, do you still believe it?" I continued questioning him.

"No, of course I don't."

"So you're telling me that you and I will never have this problem again?"

"Yes I am," Dylan agreed. And then he went into a spiel talking about how much he misses his mother and sister already. And that he wished that he hadn't gone to jail because that time could've been spent them. He even apologized to me after accusing me of not telling him that Bruce was abusing his mother. "I know you felt like you meant well by not telling me what was going on with my mother. But please don't keep anything else from me, okay?" He said.

"Okay," I said, even though I wasn't sure if I meant it or not. Besides that, it felt good to hear his apology. He sat next to me for a few more minutes and then he stood up and told me that he was about to jump into the shower because he had a few things to take care of today. As he started walking away from me, I started feeling guilty about keeping all my run-ins with Kendrick a secret. I knew I needed to tell him now or hear his mouth later. "I've got something to tell you." I got up the gumption to say. He stopped in his tracks and turned around to face me. He gave me his undivided attention. "What's up?" He asked me.

"You promise not to get mad?" I asked him, trying to gage his body language and his mental stability.

Dylan stood there with a straight look on his face. "Just say it," he replied like he was getting impatient with me.

"When I was out looking for you last night, I ran into Kendrick."

Dylan took a few steps towards me. "Did he say something to you?" Dylan looked like he was about to lose all of his marbles.

"No, he didn't. I was driving down the strip and he and another guy rode right past me and just looked at me. He stared at me until I made a right turn at the next corner and drove out of his sight."

"Yo' Kira, I swear if that motherfucker says something to you or gets close to you I want you to call me ASAP." Dylan instructed me.

"That's not his first time rolling up on me like that."

"What the fuck you mean that wasn't his first time rolling up on you?" Dylan wanted me to explain.

"While you were locked up, he pulled up on me at the gas station across the street from the police precinct and then he showed up in the parking garage when I was leaving one day."

"See this is what I be talking about. This dude doesn't have any respect for me whatsoever because if he did he wouldn't have ran up on you like that." Dylan roared. He looked like he was about to lose his damn mind. And if Kendrick were in this apartment with us right now, Dylan would put a slug in his head without hesitation. "Tell me how that fucker knows where we live?"

"Baby I don't know. Maybe he followed us home one day. Who knows?"

"So what did he say to you when he saw you in the parking garage?"

"All he said was that he knew you were locked up for shooting my dad." I replied nonchalantly.

"That's it? That's all he said?" Dylan asked, like he didn't believe me.

"Yes,"

"Nah, I don't believe that. I know this dude like the back of my hands. He said something else." Dylan grilled me for answers. He knew I was holding something back.

"So, he didn't mention anything about how Nick and I are taking all his fucking customers because they're complaining about how he keeps watering down his dope?"

"No Dylan, he didn't mention anything about that."

"Well, what did he say when he rolled up on you at the gas station?" Dylan asked. He wasn't going to leave this subject alone until I told him everything.

I hesitated for a moment and then I said, "Well, while I was pumping gas in my car he and another guy drove up behind me and told me to come here. So, when I walked up to the car he pushed a gun in my side and threatened to shoot me if I didn't tell him what I told Detective Grimes in the interrogation room before I walked out of the police station."

"He did what?" Dylan turned completely red but I could still see the green veins bursting out the side of his temples.

I was afraid to say another word. I wasn't sure if he was going to hit me or what. I refused to go through another episode of his erratic behavior. I was getting enough of that from Kendrick. "Kira, that piece of shit pointed a gun at you and threatened to shoot you?" Dylan roared.

"Yes, he threatened to shoot me if I didn't tell him what I told the cops. He thinks that I told Detective Grimes that he was the one that kill Judge Mahoney and his wife." I explained further.

"I don't give a damn about what he thought you said. I'm gonna murder that motherfucker because he threatened to kill you!" He argued, spit flew out of his mouth with every word he uttered and then he started pacing back and forth on the living room floor.

"Dylan, I know you're mad but you know you can't do anything to him right now. The cops are on our ass, so they are bound to find out if you do anything to him." I said, trying to reason with them.

"Do you think I give a damn about going back to jail? He threatened to kill you Kira.

And he pointed a gun at you. Do you know how that makes me look?" Dylan yelled and then he turned towards the wall in the living room and punched a hole in it with his fist.

I nearly jumped in the back of the sofa. The man with the erratic behavior surfaced again. "Dylan, if you go out there and kill him, then who's going to be out here with me?"

Dylan started pacing the living room floor. "I can't worry about that right now." He screeched, his voice ricocheted off the walls like thunder. "I can't let niggas like him walk around these streets talking about what they did to my wife and I don't do anything about it. I wouldn't be able to live around here."

"Well, let's move. I think it's time for us to relocate anyway." I suggested.

"And go where? This is my hometown. I'm not letting no motherfucker run me out of my town." He protested.

"So what are we gonna stay here for the rest of our lives? I mean, it's not like we have family here anymore."

"Kira, I don't care what you say, I'm not leaving. I won't give that motherfucker the satisfaction of thinking that he ran me out on my own town. And besides, Kendrick needs to get dealt with once and for all. His time on the streets as expired. And when I get rid of him, I ain't gotta worry about him fucking with you and I ain't gotta share drug turfs anymore. I'll be killing two birds with one stone."

"Look I know he's gotta be eliminated, but will you promise me that you'll get someone else to do it?" I tried to bargain with them.

"I'm sorry but I can't promise you that."

"Well would you at least think about it? I mean, you know a lot of people that want Kendrick dead. So if you get one of them to do it, then no one can point the things back at you. I swear, I can't lose you again. I have made a lot of sacrifices for you, and you know the sacrifices that I made. So I refuse to throw all that away, because you want to prove a point. You follow me?"

By this time, Dylan had stopped pacing the floor. Instead he stood next to the wall he punched a hole in like he was pondering what I had just said. This was a good sign.

After he stood there for what seemed like 1 and a half minutes, he finally turned around and left. I watched him as he headed into our bedroom. Immediately after he slammed the bedroom door shut, my heart started beating rapidly because I knew I'd just started a war between Dylan and Kendrick. I also knew that it was nothing I could say that would prevent Dylan from killing Kendrick. I just wished I'd never said anything. It would kill me inside if Kendrick killed Dylan before Dylan had a chance to kill him first. How would I continue on with my life? I'm so tired of everyone dying around me, which is why I want to get out of this town and never come back. I can only hope that Dylan finds it in his heart to listen to me because I only want the best for us. I guess time will tell.

I'm A Grown Ass Man

DYLAN

I can't fucking believe that Kira wants me to let Kendrick walk around town like he didn't violate her. Was she out of her fucking mind? Even if she wasn't, my pride wouldn't let me act like nothing hadn't happened between Kendrick and Kira. Kendrick has to be dealt with once and for all. And if his homeboys want to get in the middle then they can. They just need to know that I'm not taking any prisoners. Every body is dying and there will be no compromises.

As soon as I walked into the bathroom I turned on the shower so the water could warm up before I got in it. I took my clothes off and took a crap on the toilet until my insides were empty. After I finished I stepped in the bathtub and let the hot water cascade off my back while I pressed my hands against the ceramic tile on the bathroom wall. I closed my eyes and started thinking about my mom and my sister. I tried to think about the good times we had doing the Christmas and Thanksgiving holidays. My mother was always happy when my sister and I spent time with her. She used to always thank us for being in her life. She and my sister both were beautiful people on the inside and out. So to hear that a monster like Bruce killed her makes me think about doing evil things to grimey ass people who don't deserve to be on this earth. If I find out that those motherfuckers from the Terrace are fucking me over, I'm going to cut off every finger attached to their hands and then I'm going to cut out their tongue. Who knows, I may cut off their fucking feet too. This will send a clear message to all the hustlers in the street that they cannot fuck with my money and get away with it. Cutting a motherfucker's tongue out of their mouth, sends the message that yes, they robbed me but they won't walk around and talk about it. And chopping off a motherfucker's fingers, says yes, he stole from me but he won't steal from anyone else. And last, when you chop off a motherfucker's foot, say yes, he did me dirty but he won't walk out of my trap house and go set up shop anywhere else. When you're working in someone's dope spot, you gotta go by their rules. And when you don't, get ready to face the consequences.

I Just Started a War

KIRA

I waited a few minutes before I got off the sofa. I walked over to our bedroom door to see if I could hear what Dylan was doing on the other side. It was radio silent so I turned the doorknob and pushed the door open as quickly as I could. A couple seconds later, I heard the shower water running in the bathroom so I knew he was bathing. I pulled the bedroom door shut and dashed back into the living room. This was the perfect time for me to make a phone call to Nick. I grabbed my cell phone from the coffee table and dialed Nick's cell phone number. Thankfully he answered on the second ring. "Yo' Kira, what's up?" He asked.

"Where are you right now?"

"I'm out handling business. Why? Whatcha' need?"

"Dylan knows that Kendrick has been fucking with me. And he's not going to let it go."

"Do you blame him?"

"No I don't. But there's a right way to do stuff. So I'm gonna need you to talk to him."

"Where is he?"

"He's taking a shower right now."

"Is everything good between y'all?"

"He came home and apologized to me for how he treated me last night. So, everything started going in the right direction but then I messed things up by opening my big ass mouth."

"You know this is not going away anytime soon, right?"

"Don't remind me."

"Just keep your cool around there. And give him some time and everything will go back to normal."

"I hope you're right." I said.

Dylan got out the shower about fifteen minutes later. It took him another fifteen minutes to get dressed and when he walked back into the living room where I was still sitting, he told me he had some running around to do and that he'd see me later.

"What time are you coming back?" I asked him. I needed to know what kind of moves he was about to make. I was hoping he wouldn't tell me that he was going to pay Kendrick a visit, but then again something on the inside of me wanted to know. I figured if I knew I could possibly talk him out of doing something that he'd regret later. But who was I fooling? Dylan has turned into a different man since he got the news that his mother and sister were murdered. He's become unpredictable and unstable and I don't like that. I can't live with a man that I'm afraid of and don't trust. What kind of relationship could I have with this type of person? I know one thing, if Dylan doesn't pull it together and come back to reality, he's going to wake up one morning and I will be gone.

Time To Check On My Dope Spot

DYLAN

I got Nick on the phone as soon as I hopped in my car and sped out of the parking garage. "Yo Nick, where you at?" I asked him.

"Not too far. Why? What's up?"

"I'm on my way to the Terrace spot. So, I want you to meet me there."

"How long will it take you to get there?" He asked me.

"Probably about 20 minutes."

"A'ight, well I guess I'll see you when I get there." Nick said and then we ended the call.

I started rehearsing what I was going to say to those niggas after I walked into the dope spot. I want to go in there with the facial expression of a man who's not there to play games. I want to intimidate them to the point where they start telling on each other. And when you get them like that, you gain all the control in that situation.

Kira thought she was being slick by asking me where I was on my way to. She knew I wasn't going to tell her. So I don't know why she even asked me in the first place. Keeping your significant other out of the business you handle away from home, is how a real hustler is supposed to carry himself. Now don't get me wrong, there has been a time where I had to involve Kira, but other than that, I keep my business in the streets.

The Terrace apartments are 17 minutes away from my apartment. So, it didn't surprise me when I pulled up in front of the building and Nick wasn't there. I grabbed my cell phone from the cup holder so I could call him. But before the phone started ringing, I saw Nick driving towards me so I disconnected the call.

"I was just getting ready to call you." I yelled out the window.

Nick smiled. "Have some patience." He said while he was parking his truck alongside my car.

I grabbed my 9mm Glock from underneath the driver seat, stuck it in the waist section of my jeans and then I stepped out of my car. "You strapped?" Nick asked me.

"Of course I am, I couldn't see it any other way."

"I got my burner too, just in case these motherfuckers wanna play Cowboys and Indians."

"Did you tell those niggas that we were stopping by?" I wanted to know.

"Nah, I didn't tell 'em shit! I thought it would be better if we stopped by unannounced that way we could catch 'em with their pants down." Nick explained.

"Well, let's go." I said and then we headed up to the apartment.

The Terrace was a duplex apartment building with four units. The two units upstairs belonged Nick and I, while the two units downstairs were rented to two low-income women with kids. We knew both women. One of them was named Tasha and the other chick's name was Dakota. Nick and I had them both on the payroll. They held onto the re-up packages that our dope spots would need if and when they ran out of product. Dakota was standing outside in front of her apartment when Nick and I approached the building.

Dakota was a fairly attractive 26-year-old with a nice body. She sort of put me in the mind of Kim Kardashian because she had ass for days. But she didn't carry herself like Kim K. would. I think women are supposed to look presentable at all times. Dakota didn't look at it that way. She'd rather walk around outside with a pair of sweatpants on, a pair of bedroom shoes and a bonnet on her head. And that's not how a woman is supposed to walk around. Other than that, she's a sweet young girl and she looks out for our spot. "What brings you two around these parts?" She smiled and asked.

"We just wanted to come out here to make sure everything was running smoothly." Nick said.

"It's been kind of quiet out here." She mentioned.

"Whatcha' mean by that?" I interjected.

"The dope fiends haven't been coming through. I still got the same stuff Nick dropped off to me four days ago." She replied. "Monty tried to get me to give it to him the day before yesterday, but I told him no. I told him that he knew how shit worked. When he gives me the money from the other package, then he could get the new shit. So he walked away fussing and calling me all kinds of bitches. So I told him to stop crying and take care of his business and then he can get it."

"Where is that nigga now?" Nick asked her.

"I think he's upstairs."

"What about Roman? Is he upstairs too?"

"Yeah, I think so."

"Have you heard anything about them niggas diluting my dope?" I asked her.

"I heard something like that. But you really can't go off the word of a dope fiend because none of their tolerant levels are the same."

"Where's Tasha?" Nick wanted to know.

"She just left to drop both of her kids off at her mom's house."

"Where's your little girl?" Nick's questions continued.

"She's in the house taking a nap. She's at that terrible two age so she's getting badder by the day."

"When she wakes up, take her to go get some ice cream." Nick suggested as he handed her a $100 bill.

"Thank you!" She replied with excitement while she stuffed the $100 bill down into her pants pocket.

Nick and I excused ourselves and headed upstairs to have a talk with Monty and Roman.

Before we could reach the top step and knock on the door, Roman unlocked and opened it. “What a pleasant surprise?” Roman said.

I didn't crack a smile and neither did Nick. Instead we pushed the door back so we could have enough room to cross the entryway. Roman stepped to the side. “Where is Monty?” I asked Roman, as I stood toe to toe with him. I looked straight into his eyes and did not flinch one bit.

“He's in the back.” Roman replied.

“Go take a seat.” I instructed him. And as soon he walked away, I took a couple of steps forward so Nick could close the door behind us and lock it. “Monty bring your ass out here.” I roared.

Nick stood alongside of me while I stood in the middle floor. A couple of seconds later Monty finally joined us. I gave him the look of death when he appeared from around the corner. “What's up?” He asked. He seemed a bit nervous like he didn't know whether to smile or look serious.

“Have a seat.” Nick instructed him.

After Monty took a seat next to Roman, I let the cat out of the bag. “So, what’s going on with the package? Why ain’t it gon yet?”

Monty spoke up first. "It's been slow. I guess ain't nobody got no money."

"How much dope y'all got left?" I asked them both.

"We got like $6,000 worth."

"So, y'all got $4,000?" I pressed the issue.

"Yeah," Monty said and reached down in his pocket and pulled out a folded knot of 5, 10 and 20-dollar bills. He handed me the money. I handed it to Nick so he could count it.

"Tell me why you went to Dakota and asked her to give you the dope package she has when you know you aren't supposed to get it until you give her the money from the last package first?" I asked him.

"She's a fucking liar. I didn't ask her for shit." Monty spat. He stood on his feet like he wanted to leave the apartment to confront Dakota.

But I stopped him in his tracks. "Where the fuck are you going? Sit your ass down until I tell you to get up." I roared.

Monty took a seat that instant, while Nick handed the money back to me. "It's $500 short." Nick told me. So, I immediately turned my focus back towards Monty.

"I thought you said that this was four grand." I huffed. This guy was making me lose patience with him.

Monty looked at Nick. "You sure it's not four grand?" He asked him.

"Monty, don't play motherfucking games with me! You know–you only have $3,500." Nick snapped.

Monty looked at Roman. "Roman, didn't I have four grand on me?" Monty asked him. He hoped that Roman would throw him a life jacket but that didn't happen.

"I don't know. You always keep the money on you." Roman explained. It became apparent that Monty was doing some misdeeds with the drugs and the money and now it was starting to catch up with him.

"Where is the dope?" I asked them both.

"It's in the refrigerator." Monty spoke.

"Roman, go in the kitchen and get it." I said.

Roman stood up from the sofa and headed to the kitchen. He came back 1 minute and a half later with the zip lock bag of my product. "Give it to me." I instructed him.

After Roman handed me the Zip lock bag of dope, I inspected it. I turned it over at least 3 times. "This don't look like 6 grand worth of dope. This looks like 4 grand worth." I protested. "Nick look at this shit and tell me what you think." I said and handed Nick the clear plastic bag.

Nick inspected it by turning the bag around twice and then he opened it up and sifted his fingers through the little small packages of powder. "You're right. This looks like it's about 3 to 4 grand worth of work."

"Where's the rest of my dope Monty?" I asked him, trying to remain calm. I knew that if he said something that I didn't like there was a huge chance that I was going to kill him or hurt him really bad.

"Well, since it's been slow, I gave this nigga name Papoose some work so I could hurry up and get rid of it." Monty tried to explain.

"You gave a nigga I don't know some of my product so he could hurry up and get rid of it?" I roared. I saw the way Nick was watching me through my peripheral vision. He knew my state of mind so he stepped up and said, "Come here Monty, let me talk to you for a minute." Nick intervened.

While Nick took Monty outside I stood there and turned my attention towards Roman. Roman was a cool, young guy. He used to play basketball in high school and got a 4-year scholarship to play at UM, but he screwed up in his freshman year by getting caught with a pound of marijuana in his dorm room. UM kicked him out of school so he started selling drugs fulltime. The little dude reminds me of Allen Iverson. "What's up with Monty? Is he stepping on my dope?" I didn't hesitate to ask him.

"Dylan man, I don't know what be going on around here." He answered me. But he acted like he was holding something back. So I took a couple steps towards him and leaned forward in his direction. "Look Roman, I know you don't wanna be labeled as a snitch. But if you don't tell me what the fuck is going on around here, I'm gonna treat you like one." I threatened him.

His facial expression changed instantly. "Look Dee, Monty runs this spot. Whatever he tells me to do I do it."

"What did he tell you to do?"

"He told me to help him dump out all the packs of dope onto a plate and add some cut to it. He said if we add the right amount of cut, we could still sell the dope and make more money in the process. So, I helped him. But after we added the cut to it, the fiends started complaining saying the dope wasn't good so we got stuck with it."

"Is it true that he gave some of the dope to a nigga named Papoose?"

"Dee, I don't know who the hell he's talking about. I think he made up that name."

I swear my blood started boiling at a high temperature. To find out that this nigga Monty was fucking up my business made me so angry that I could feel the veins in my arms protruding through my skin. Why insult my intelligence? Why bite the hand that feeds him? Have I not been good to that ungrateful motherfucker? Have I not shown this motherfucker nothing but love? I guess all of that is about to end. I'm done fucking with that piece of shit. He's out of here today.

"Roman, I'm gonna take this dope with me. But I'm gonna get Dakota to give you the other package. So, handle your business and make things right because you're in charge now."

"Are you really putting me in charge?" He asked me.

"What about Monty?"

"Don't worry about Monty. Today is his last day." I told Roman, who was by the way looking somewhat puzzled.

"Am I gonna run this spot by myself?" Roman wanted to know.

"Yeah, but don't worry. Nick is gonna bring my little dude Man-Man over here to take Monty's place." I assured him. "So, are you good?" I continued, while searching his face for any sign of weakness.

"Yeah, I'm good," he replied.

"You gotcha' burner with you?"

"Yep, I got it right here." Roman said, as he pulled his shirt up. I could see the handle of the gun sticking out the waist area of his jeans.

"I hope you got the safety on. Don't want you shooting your dick off." I commented giving him a half smile.

Roman chuckled. "Yeah it's on safety."

"A'ight, well I'm going to get out of here, so make me proud and get that money."

"I don't know how to get it any other way."

"My man…." I said and then I exited the apartment.

When I walked downstairs, I noticed that Dakota was still standing outside of her apartment, while Nick and Monty stood by his truck. I could see them talking but I couldn't hear what they were saying.

"You're leaving already?" She said.

"Yeah, but listen, take that package upstairs to Roman because he's out of product."

"Is he giving me money?"

"Nah, I've already collected the dough from Monty. But check this out, I want you to look out for Roman because he's gonna be here by himself for the rest of today. Nick is going to bring a new dude over here named Man-Man. He's gonna take Monty's place. So keep your eyes and ears open and let me know if anything doesn't look right."

"You know I'm on it." She expressed as she smiled.

After I was done talking to Dakota I walked over to where Nick and Monty were standing. "Monty, get in the truck with Nick and Nick I want you to follow me." I instructed them both.

I got back into my car and pulled out into the road. A couple of seconds later Nick followed suit. A million things started running through my mind concerning Monty. One part of me wanted to kill him and throw him into the ocean. But the smart side of me said to live and let live. I can't say which part of me I should listen to, but I knew some type of consequence had to happen. Hopefully, I can get Nick to help me make that decision.

I Never Listen To Anyone

KIRA

Dylan never wants me to leave the apartment but I got shit to do. I mean if I had to wait on him to do things for me, they wouldn't get done in a timely manner. So today, I decided to make a run to the supermarket about three miles up the block. I figured since my list was small I could go in and come out in last than ten minutes. Maybe in even less time, who knows?

Before I could get out of my apartment good my cell phone started ringing. I retrieved it from my purse and looked at the caller ID. I didn't recognize the phone number so I hesitated to answer it. After the fifth ring, I finally decided to answer the call. "Hello," I said.

"Hello Kira, this is Mr. Glasser."

"Who?" I asked, trying to jog my memory.

"Your father's estate attorney."

"Oh, I'm sorry. I didn't recognize your voice."

"Oh, no need for that. I was calling to see if I could stop by your place today."

"What's wrong?"

"Nothing is wrong. I just need to execute your father's last will and testament."

"What time are you talking?"

"I have an appointment at 1 o'clock. So, I'm thinking maybe two?"

I thought for a moment while I looked at the time on my microwave oven. It was already a few minutes after 12:00, so was I really in the mood to have him stop by my apartment after such short notice?

"Kira, are you there?" Mr. Glasser asked. He probably thought I disconnected our phone call because the airways between both phones went completely silent.

"Yes, I'm still up here. I'm just trying to figure out how to accommodate you and run my errands at the same time." I lied. Truth is, I didn't want to meet anyone that was associated with my father. I know Mr. Glasser is saying that he wants to come by and read my father's will, but he could have a hidden agenda. Detective Grimes could have him coming to my apartment to spy on me, which is why I need to stay on my toes. I can't let these guys outsmart me because if that ever happens, I can kiss my freedom goodbye.

"I'll tell you what, just give me 5 or 10 minutes to read your father's will and then I'll be out of your hair." He pressed the issue.

I hesitated for a second and then I said, "Okay, if you come by my apartment at 2 o'clock, you'll be out of here by 2:10?"

"Yes, I will." He assured me.

"Alright, I'll see you at 2."

"Sounds great. See you then." He replied and then he hung up.

After I put my cell phone back into my purse, I rushed out of my apartment so I could get to the store and back home before Dylan. With Kendrick threatening to do something to me, it would devastate Dylan if he came home and I wasn't here. I know his only goal is to protect me, but I'm not new to the streets. I've done everything under the sun, from whipping bitches' asses to robbing big time drug dealers and most recently I killed my father for him, so he could give me some kind of credit because I've earned it.

Getting Rid of the Dead Weight

DYLAN

Nick followed me for ten miles to our destination, which was an old trap house I used to stash my product in about 6 months ago. Now dope fiends use it as a shooting gallery. I pulled up in front of the house and motioned for Nick to get out of his truck and come and get in my car. While he did it, Monty stayed back and watched. He had a worried look on his face. He wasn't naïve. He knew something was about to happen to him. He just didn't know what it was.

"I want you to take this dope and get rid of it." I said to Nick immediately after he got into my car and closed the door.

"Whatcha' want me to do with the dope?"

"Take it and go mix it up so we can get all the extra cut off of it. Then repackage it so we can put it back on the street."

"Whatcha' want me to do with him?" Nick asked me, looking at Monty for a second and then he looked back at me.

"Kill 'em. I can't have a nigga robbing me and smiling in my face at the same time. We need to make an example out of him."

"Nah Dylan, right now isn't a good time to drop another body. Remember we've got a lot of heat on us because of those other murders. I just think that we should beat him up really good. You know, knock some teeth out and break his arms."

"That's not good enough. We got to make him pay for what he did. Do you know that Roman said that Monty didn't give the dope to a nigga name Papoose? And he said that Monty doesn't even know a nigga with that name." I pointed out. I needed Nick to see where I was going with this conversation.

"Listen Dylan, you know I'm down with anything you tell me, but I think we should send a message to Monty another way. Just trust me on this one." Nick pleaded.

I thought about what Nick said for a moment and then I said, "A'ight, take 'em over to Rich's spot and tell them to do everything but kill him."

"Got it." Nick said and then he gave me a handshake.

I watched Nick as he drove away. I'm sure Monty is wondering what's about to happen with him. Deep in the back of his mind I know he thinks he's about to get murked. If it were up to me he would, but since I'm gonna go with Nick's judgment call, he's going to live to see another day.

Leave Me Alone

KIRA

Mr. Glasser who was my father's estate attorney stopped by my apartment so we could go over my dad's will. I really wished that we could've put this off for another day, but the guy suggested that we needed to do it now. "How are you?" He asked me after I opened my front door to let him in.

"I'm trying to make it." I told him.

"Well, you look well." He complimented me.

"Thank you. You can sit over there on the sofa." I replied while I closed and locked my front door.

"Are you ready for me to read your father's will?" He asked me after he took a seat and placed his briefcase on the coffee table.

"I guess so," I told him while I took a seat on the chair next to the coffee table.

He took a file from his briefcase, laid it down in front of him and then he smiled. "Well let's do it."

I sat there quietly as Mr. Glasser started reading my father's last will and testament. The beginning of the document was pretty generic with standard legal jargon, but halfway through it things started getting interesting. "To my only child, Kira Lynise Wade, I leave you my home, worth 1.5 million, the money in my bank accounts and IRAs totaling a sum of 2.3 million, my Porshe', which is valued at $140,000, and last my investment property in Colorado State."

I was stunned because I couldn't believe that my father had all this money and property. But what was eating away at me was the fact that I'm gaining all of his money and possessions, from a man I killed. I swear I felt so sick to my stomach. I didn't deserve any of this. So what do I do? Do I tell Mr. Glasser that I can accept all this stuff? Or do I tell him to give it to charity? But then, what if I tell him to give it to charity and he starts looking at me really weird? Will that be a red flag that I had something to do with his death and now I'm feeling guilty? I guess the best thing for me to do right now is to talk to Dylan about it when he gets home.

Wake Me Up From This Nightmare

DYLAN

I called Kira and asked her to meet me at the valet area of our apartment building so she could take a ride with me to my mother's house. I could've gone there alone but I hated surprises and walking in that house and seeing something I hadn't conditioned my mind to handle, I'd probably freak out and start breaking everything in that damn house. I figured if I let Kira walk into every room before me she could forewarn me about certain things.

"You a'ight?" She asked me after she sat in my car and fastened her seatbelt.

"Nah, I'm not all right." I told her as I sped away from our apartment building.

"Do you care to talk about it?" I wondered aloud.

"Not really."

"Okay, then." She replied sarcastically and then she turned her head around and started staring out of the passenger side window.

We drove in silence for at least 2 minutes before I struck up a conversation. "What did you do while I was gone?"

"I didn't do anything."

"Has anyone tried to call you?" My questions continued.

"I talked to my father's estate attorney. He came to the apartment about an hour ago." She replied nonchalantly.

"What did he want with you?"

"He stopped by to read my father's will."

"What did it say?"

"It basically said that I get everything. The house, his car, his bank account and his investments."

"How much was in his bank account?"

"It's close to 2 million."

"He had that much money in his account?" I pressed the issue. I had no idea that that old man was sitting on all that money."

"That dollar amount is a mixture of investments and cash."

"Have you thought about what you're gonna do with the house?"

"No I haven't." She began to say, "I'm still trying to come to terms that he's dead." She continued.

"Well, he is, so deal with it." I told her. I need her to toughen up. She's not the only one who lost a parent. I did too. And now that that has happened we need to figure out how to take care of our business and move on.

"Why do you have to be so insensitive?" She griped.

"Because we live in a cold world and if I don't prepare you now, you're going to get swallowed up in the streets." I explained.

"Do you think that I am that naïve? Do you think that you are the only dealer I've ever been with? I come from the streets. I've transported drugs before. I know how to cook crack. And I know how to fire a gun. So don't come at me like I'm some little girl that was born yesterday because I could probably get more gangster than you can." She spat.

I looked at her and smiled. "So you think you gangsta, huh?"

"Dylan, don't fuck with me because I'm not in the mood for your shit today!"

I had to laugh again. Kira was definitely trying to throw her weight around. So, I sat there and paid attention.

"Are you done?" I asked her.

"Dylan, just leave me alone please. You're giving me a headache."

"As you wish." I said and turned my attention to the road in front of me.

Twisted Behavior

KIRA

Dylan walked inside his mother's home first while I followed. There was forensic yellow tape all over the place. The air inside the house was cold. The energy in the house felt creepy too. It had been a while since I'd been inside this house, so it felt weird that when I was finally able to gain access to it, no one was here.

Before we left the police station, Detective Grimes told us that Bruce's body was found in the master bedroom, so we went to that part of the house first. Upon entering the bedroom, Dylan stepped to the side so I could lead the way. It only took me about 5 footsteps into the bedroom before I was able to see the huge blood stained carpet on the left side of the bed. I assumed that this was where Bruce shot himself.

"This is where he shot himself." I told Dylan while I pointed to the area.

Dylan shook his head in disgust as he looked over my shoulders. "That coward got off scott free." He said.

"Trust me, he didn't get off scott free. His ass is going straight to hell!" I interjected.

"But, I wanted to do it. I wanted to be the one that took his last breath." Dylan roared. I immediately saw his eyes tear up. And before I could blink an eye, Dylan broke down and started crying. "I can't believe that that motherfucker killed my mother and my sister. What did they ever do to him? My mother married this nigga and let him move into my father's house. And this is how he repays her?" He continued sobbing.

I reached over and pulled Dylan into my arms. I tried to hold him as tightly as I could. Seeing him hurt like this really bothered me. Dylan wasn't the type of man that would cry. He has always played the macho role, which is why I am glad that I came here with him. He probably would've lost his mind if he had come here alone.

"Why did he have to do this to them? They never bothered anyone. They were good people." Dylan pointed out.

"Baby, I know they were. And that's why they're in heaven." I tried to console him.

"Fuck that! I want them here!" He snapped and broke away from my embrace.

I stood there trying to figure out what to do next. Should I try to hug him again? Or should I just stand there and let him vent? "I want them here too." I said, in a calm tone, hoping this situation here would end peacefully.

Dylan took a seat at the foot of the bed. I stood in front of him while he buried his face in the palms of his hands. "Kira, what am I going to do without them?" he sobbed.

"We're gonna have to take this one day at a time." I suggested.

"What about my sister? We gotta get the news to her husband."

"I know we do. Just let me handle that."

"What about this house? What are we going to do with it?"

I sighed heavily. "We'll figure it out." I told him. But in reality, I didn't want to figure it out. I have my own issues with my father's estate. Trying to wrap my mind around his family issues and my father's stuff was starting to give me a headache. It seemed like the pressure was mounting at a fast rate. At one point I felt like I couldn't breath. I also couldn't think straight. So what do we do, runaway from our problems and never look back? I would love to do just that, but Dylan wouldn't hear of it.

Dylan and I stayed in his mother's bedroom for about 3 minutes and then I encouraged him to walk through the rest of the house. “Let's go to the other bedroom and then let’s go back downstairs to check out the living room and kitchen area.” I said and then I grabbed his hand and pulled him up from the bed.

It didn't take us long to walk through the other bedroom. Nothing looked out of place so we peeked in the bathroom and then we headed back downstairs. Like upstairs, everything was clean and in place so we took a seat at the bar area of the kitchen. “I wish I could turn back the hands of time.” Dylan said, while he was staring down at the kitchen floor.

“Don't we all.” I commented.

“Do you know that I was the one that introduced Bruce to my mother?”

Shocked by his confession, I looked at him and said, “No, I didn’t.”

“Well, yeah I was the one. I remember meeting him at the gun range a couple years ago. It seemed like every time I was there he would pop up. So one day we were talking and he mentioned that his wife died of cancer a few years prior, so to stay preoccupied, he would either go fishing or come to the shooting range. So I come up with the bright idea of introducing him to my mama and I invited him to come to a barbecue we had. And when he showed up I introduced him to mama, they hit it off really well. So one thing led to another, they started dating and a year later they got married. I even paid for the fucking wedding, because I was so happy that she was happy and that she wasn't going to be alone anymore. But I guess, I fucked that up, huh?"

"Don't beat yourself up about it. This could have happened to anyone."

"Don't you get it? If I hadn't introduced that motherfucker to my mother, she would be alive right now." He snapped.

I wanted to intervene with hopes of calming him down, but I didn't. I was sensing a pattern of his passive aggressive behavior. It wouldn't shock me is he was diagnosed with a bipolar disorder. He would go from one extreme to the next in a matter of seconds. "I need to figure out how I'm delivering the news to Sonya's husband. He is going to have a fucking fit when he finds out that she's dead."

"Don't worry about that. I'll find out who his commanding officer is and make sure he gets the message to him." I offered.

Dylan and I went over a few more things after he calmed down a little. I helped him grab a couple of old photos of his mother, along with her important documents before we left the house. He knew he would need them when it was time to handle her affairs. I just pray that he can keep it together until then.

We Got a Problem

DYLAN

Later that day Nick called me while I was lying in bed and watching TV with Kira. It was a little after 11 o'clock when my cell phone rang. I grabbed my iPhone from the nightstand and answered it. "What's up?" I asked.

"We got a problem." He replied.

"What kind of problem are you talking about?" I wanted to know. Anxiety started consuming me while I waited for Nick to answer me. With everything going on I don't need to take on more shit. My shoulders are already heavy.

"Monty is in the hospital and the cops are there asking questions." Nick told me.

"Look, don't say another word. Where are you?" I asked him.

"I'm over here by Dakota's spot."

"Stay there. I'll be there in fifteen minutes." I said and then I ended the call.

"What's wrong?" Kira asked me while she watched me climb out of the bed.

"Nick fucked up really bad!" I told her while I slipped on a pair of sweatpants that I grabbed from my dresser drawer.

"What did he do?" Her questions continued.

"Didn't you hear me tell him not to say another word?" I spat.

"Yeah,"

"Well, then that means that I can't answer your question." I replied sarcastically. Kira was beginning to get on my fucking nerves with the questions. I'm already aggravated. I just wished that she would take a back seat and let me do shit my way.

I thought she was going to say something else, but she didn't. I was glad too. So, after I slipped on my sneakers, I put on a fitted cap, grabbed my car keys and headed for the front door. "Don't wait up for me." I yelled.

"Who said I was?" I heard her say. I knew then that she was pissed off with me. I'll just apologize to her later. But right now, I've got more pressing things that need to be fixed.

When I pulled up to the spot, Nick was standing outside talking to Dakota and Tasha in front of the duplex. As soon as I hopped out of my car Nick started walking towards me. We met each other midway. "What the fuck is going on?" I didn't hesitate to ask him.

"I got Rich and Man-Man to rough Monty up a bit. Well, after they did, I heard Monty ended up with two broken legs, one broken arm and a fractured skull. And right now, he's in the hospital having emergency surgery." Nick explained.

"Who told you?"

"Tasha and Dakota knows his baby mama. They said that the police is at the hospital right now talking to her."

"See, I knew we should've killed that nigga!" I hissed. I was becoming enraged by this bullshit I was hearing. Only if this nigga Nick would've listened to me, we wouldn't be out here having this conversation. But no, he thought it was best to spare the nigga Monty. Now the cops are swarming around the fucking emergency room trying to find out who hurt him. What a fucked up night!

"Look Dylan, I know you're pissed off. But I'm gonna get the word to his baby mama that if she tells the cops anything that she's going to get it too."

"So, that's it? You think by sending her a threatening message that it's going to stop her from talking to the cops?" I replied sarcastically. This plan of his was fucking stupid and generic. If it were up to me I will kill Monty, his baby mama and the rest of his family. Leave no witnesses alive.

"Listen Dee, I only called you so you wouldn't be left in the dark. But I'm gonna handle this. I'm gonna take care of everything."

"You better because I can't have any more slip-ups."

"A'ight," Nick said.

"So what's going on with Roman? Is he handling things up stairs?" I questioned Nick.

"Yeah, he's almost out of the stuff Dakota gave him earlier today."

"Does he know what happened to Monty?"

"If he does he hasn't said anything about it."

"Good. Try to keep it from him, at least until you get that message to his baby mama."

"Does Dakota and Tasha know that Man-Man and Rich did it?"

"No I don't think so."

"Good. Keep it that way. The less people that know about it the better off we'll be."

Nick shook his head like he was holding something back from me. "What's up? You got something to tell me?" I continued. I was feeling uneasy by the way he was acting all of a sudden.

"Right before I dropped Monty off to Rich and Man'Man's spot, I rode by Kendrick and a couple of his workers."

"You saw them by Man-Man and Rich's spot?" I asked. I needed some clarity.

"No, I saw them at the stop light at the corner of Old Dixie and Jefferson Street. I was on one side of the street and he was on the other side.

"Did he see you?"

"Yeah, and everyone of those niggas he had with him stared me down like they wanted to do something. I'm thinking they thought that me and Monty were strapped with our pistols because instead of saying something, they just gritted on us and kept moving."

"I'm ready to kill that nigga right now." I snarled. The thought of him terrorizing my fucking fiancée makes me want to go and track him down now. But it's all-good, I will get that motherfucker back. Just wait and see.

After I wrapped things up with Nick, I hopped back in my car and headed back to my apartment. I hoped Kira would be sleep by the time I got back because I wasn't in the mood to answer any of her fucking questions. Now don't get me wrong, I love Kira and she's my ride or die chick, but lately she and I haven't been able to see eye to eye. Okay granted she killed her father for me, which of course showed me how much she loves me, but it does not negate the fact that she could've prevented my mother and sister from getting killed. Not only that, she continues to put herself in harms way by allowing that nigga Kendrick to get close to her. I bet those motherfuckers are laughing at me. They probably got all those niggas on the south side talking about me and calling me a pussy. I know one thing, they better not let me hear it because I would kill one of those bastards on sight. It would be one to the head and the other one to the chest. No questions asked.

Hopefully, after all of this is over Kira will get a better understanding about how I operate things. Okay granted, she used to do a lot of crazy shit in the streets before I met her, but I know one thing; the streets have changed some. So, the quicker she recognizes that I only want the best for her and that I wouldn't tell her anything wrong, the better off she'll be. Quiet as kept, I would turn into a basket case if something ever happened to her. I would kill whoever killed her and then I'd go after their family members. I would kill everybody from the grandmother to the niece and nephew. I'd even kill their dog if they had one. No one would be exempt from my wrath. Not Kendrick, his family or his homeboys. Everybody has to go.

Hopefully, after all of this is over Kira will get a better understanding about how I operate things. Okay granted, she used to do a lot of crazy shit in the streets before I met her, but I know one thing; the streets have changed a lot. So, the quicker she recognizes that I only want the best for her and that I wouldn't tell her anything wrong, the better things will get between us and then we can go back to the way we were.

No He Didn't

KIRA

Dylan came back home an hour later. I was still lying in bed watching TV when he walked back into the bedroom. I wanted to ask him what happened while he was out, but I refused to give him the satisfaction of talking shit to me again.

I watched him through my peripheral vision, as he got undressed. He took off his sneakers, t-shirt and his sweatpants. A few minutes later, he slid back in the bed and then he turned over on his side with his back facing me. I knew this meant that he didn't want to be bothered and that he was going to sleep, so once again I left him alone.

The following morning, I woke up with my stomach growling so I went to the kitchen to eat a bowl of my favorite cereal, Frosted Rice Krispies. While I was down to my last bite, Dylan decides to stroll into the kitchen. I avoided eye contact with him. He noticed and said, "So, you're not gonna say good morning?"

"What's so good about it?"

"Oh, so you're mad about last night?" He asked.

"Don't ask me any stupid questions." I replied spastically.

"What's so stupid about it?"

"Do you remember how you talked to me last night?" I snapped. I swear this guy was really starting to get on my nerves and his mood swings were starting to become unbearable.

"Do you remember the question you asked me?"

"This conversation is useless. So, just forget it." I said and than I got up from the kitchen table.

"Where you going?" He inquired after I placed my cereal bowl and spoon in the kitchen sink and headed out of the kitchen.

"Don't ask me any more questions." I told him and disappeared around the corner.

I thought Dylan was going to follow me down the hall, which is something that he would always do when we were having a heated discussion, but this time but he didn't. Something is off with Dylan. I know he just lost his family but why carry me through the motions unnecessarily. I've been down with this guy since day one and this is the thanks I get? How dare he treat me like a fucking chick in the street? I just murdered my father for him so for God's sake will he acknowledge it and start treating me better than he has these last couple of days? That's not asking for too much. I just wish he would get with the program.

Since I had no plans to go anywhere, I crawled back into my bed and started binging on one of Netflix original series. I started watching the series called Stranger Things. And while I was in the middle of the first episode, Dylan casually made his way back into our bedroom. I was lying on my back with two pillows propped up behind my head when he made his public apology. "I'm sorry for the way I talked to you last night. And I promise it won't happen again." He's said as he stood at the foot of our bed.

I gave him a blank stare. He had no idea how I was going to react after I mustered up this facial expression. I stared at him for a few more seconds without saying one word. He didn't like the way things were going so he said, "Do you forgive me or not?"

"I want to forgive you but every time I do it, you always turn around and do the same thing over again."

"That's because you always catch me at a bad time." He tried to explain.

"So that's the only excuse you can come up with?"

"I don't know what else you want me to say."

"I want you to apologize and mean it."

"I just did that."

"You know what? Just forget it. This whole situation is draining me. I have done so much and just recently made a huge sacrifice to keep this relationship together but now I'm starting to have regrets."

"Did I ask you to do that?"

"What kind of question is that?" I snarled. He was beginning to get underneath my skin now.

"Just answer it." He instructed me.

"No, you didn't. But when a person needs something they shouldn't have to ask for it."

"Do you know that I would rather be in jail on an attempted murder charge than to see my family buried six feet underground? I love them with everything inside of me."

"And you don't think I loved my father?"

"That's not the question."

"Well it's my question to you. Now answer it." I demanded and then I sat up in the bed.

"Look Kira, I don't have time to stand here and argue with you."

"Well, bye!" I roared and then I pointed towards the bedroom door. Without saying another word, Dylan turned and walked out of our bedroom.

Matters of the Heart

DYLAN

I grabbed a pair of Lebron sneakers from the hall closet and then I grabbed my NY Yankee fitted ball cap and my car keys from the countertop in the kitchen and then I exited the apartment. I really had nowhere to go but I had to find something to do just so I could get out of the apartment.

Refusing to wait on one of the valet drivers to bring me my vehicle I retrieved it from the garage myself. I pressed the Unlock button from my keychain and heard it chirp. Beep! Immediately after I got into the driver seat, I put the key in the ignition, started up the engine and then I sped out of the parking garage with the Migos song, "Bad & Boujee" pumping through my speakers. I bopped my head to the beat and acted like I didn't have a care in the world. But deep down inside I did. My family is dead. I'm beefing with my girlfriend, the order I made to have Monty killed was botched because of my stupid ass partner. And to add insult to injury, I got the cops breathing down my back over some murders I haven't committed. Isn't life a bitch?

I rode around for an hour just to clear my head. Trying to deal with everything I had all my plate was becoming difficult by the minute. I wasn't in the mood to eat anything but I knew the only thing that would calm me down was a drink. So I pulled up to this spot called Lush and went inside. The crowd was small, which is how I like it, so it was easy for me to find a seat at the bar and drank my sorrows away.

There where two female bartenders working. They were both white women, around the ages of 23 or 24. They were dressed in 2-piece bikinis and booty shorts. And they both seemed like they were the happiest people in the world. "Good afternoon!" One of them greeted me.

I smiled. "Good afternoon, to you too." I replied.

"What can I help you with?" She asked me.

"Can I get a shot of Effen?"

"You sure can." She said and then she placed a shot glass in front of me. She grabbed a bottle of Effen from the liquor case behind her and then she poured me a shot. I grabbed the shot glass and poured every ounce of it into my mouth. And after I swallowed it I placed the shot glass back down on the bar and asked her to refill it. Without saying a word she filled my shot glass back up and stood there to see if I was going to down it like I did the first one. So to show her that I am a big man and I can handle this, I picked the shot glass up from the bar and poured all the vodka into my mouth. Once again, after I swallowed it I sat the shot glass back down on the bar. "Do you want another one?" She asked me.

"Yeah, pour me another one, but I think this is it." I told her.

I watched her pour me another shot of Effen into my shot glass. And when she was done, she sat the bottle down on the liquor case and started making drinks for two new patrons at the bar. I scanned the entire area and noticed that I was the only black guy here. There were no familiar faces so I able to let my guard down a little bit and unwind.

After I downed my third shot of Effen, I sat there and stared at myself in the glass mirror above the liquor case. My vision was a little fuzzy from the effects of the vodka, but I saw what I needed to see. I was a handsome guy. I had the look of a wise man and I looked like I was fearless so why was my heart feeling differently? Like Kendrick, I was feared and respected in the streets. So why do I feel defenseless? Why am I feeling so disrespected? Is it because I couldn't do anything to save my mother and sister? Or is it because Kendrick was fucking with my wife while Monty was robbing me of my money and drug? Right now, I don't have the answer but it will come to me eventually.

If I Ruled the World

KIRA

Three days had past and Dylan and I were still in a bad space. He's been sleeping in the guest room and he doesn't show any sign of patching things up with me. He's also been drinking heavily and doesn't show any signs of stopping that either. I've talked to Nick about it with hopes that he could talk some sense into Dylan but those efforts have crashed and burned.

Yesterday my father's estate attorney called and told me that I needed to come by his office to sign off on the documents I would need to carry to my father's bank so I could take control of his IRA and bank accounts. But Dylan wasn't having it. So, the attorney made another trip here to our apartment today and Dylan wasn't at all accommodating. "Want something to drink?" I asked Mr. Glasser after he took a seat on the sofa.

"He's not going to be here long so why are you offering him something to drink?" Dylan asked me as he stood alongside of me. I was embarrassed for Mr. Glasser and myself that I wanted to crawl into a corner and stay there. Dylan had just come back from drinking at one of the bars just up the block. He had been making it his favorite place to go.

"Yes, he's right. All I need for you to do is sign these five documents and then I will be on my way." He said while he spread the paperwork around on the coffee table. "Do you have a pen?" I asked the poor little white man. He was acting so nervous.

"Yes, I have one right here." He said and pulled a black ballpoint pen from his briefcase. Before he instructed me to bend down and sign the papers, I sat down on the sofa next to him and waited for his direction.

"What is she signing?" Dylan asked the attorney while he continued to stand in the middle of the living room floor with his arms folded. He was acting like a fucking bodyguard. In my eyes, he was being a fucking bully.

"These are the forms I'm gonna need to change everything over from my dad's name to mines." I explained.

"I didn't ask you. I asked him?" Dylan said sarcastically.

"She's right. These are the documents she's going to need to take to her father's bank.

Once she submits this paperwork to them, she'll control all of his money, stocks, bonds and assets." Mr. Glasser told him.

I tried to avoid looking at Dylan for fear of him saying something else that would further embarrass me. I kept my focus on the paperwork on the coffee table in front of me, wishing that this moment would be up right now.

Finally after getting the paperwork in order, Mr. Glasser explained each document to me and when he got to the bottom of the page, he instructed me to sign it. The whole process took three minutes to do. And when everything was all said and done, Mr. Glasser handed me my copies and then he got up to leave. "If you need anything just call me." He told me.

"I sure will." I assured him as I escorted him to the front door.

"Good day sir," Mr. Glasser said when he looked at Dylan.

"Yeah, yeah, yeah." Dylan replied and waved Mr. Glasser off.

"Thanks again for coming by." I told him.

"No problem." He said as he made his way out of my apartment.

Following Mr. Glasser's departure, I closed and locked the door. And when I turned around to give Dylan a piece of my mind he had already turned around and started walking down the hallway towards our bedroom.

"Why the hell did you have to act like that to that man?" I asked him while I followed him down the hall.

"Look, I can do anything I want to do in my house."

"This is my fucking house too." I spat.

"Give me a fucking break!" He said and then he made a detour to the hallway bathroom. After he went inside he closed the door and locked it.

I started banging on the door with my fist. "Open the door Dylan." I demanded.

"I'm using the bathroom so beat it." He said.

"You're a fucking asshole you know that?!" I yelled and then I kicked the bottom of the door with my feet.

"I know now leave me alone." He yelled back.

"Yeah, all right. We'll see who has the last word." I commented and then I walked away from the bathroom door.

I rushed into my bedroom, slipped on a pair of Prada flip-flops, grabbed my Celine' handbag from the doorknob of my closet door and then I raced towards the front door. Dylan was still in the bathroom when I scurried by it. By the time I opened the front door I heard Dylan when he flushed the toilet stool. "Come on Kira, we gotta' get out of here." I said, giving myself a pep talk.

After the door was completely ajar, I stepped across the threshold and then I turned around to pull the door close. "Well, good afternoon." I heard a voice say to me from behind. They startled the hell out of me. This sudden distraction forced me to turn around to see who was behind that voice. And when I turned around and saw that it was my neighbor Molly, I quickly spoke to her and then I turned my attention back to the front door. "On your way out?" She questioned me while I was locking the front door.

"Yes, I am."

"Okay great, me too. So, I guess we can share an elevator.

"I'm not taking the elevator. I'm going to the garage to pick up my own car." I told her.

"Oh, what a pitty! I wanted to talk to you."

"We can do it another time?" I told her, even though I wouldn't dare sit down and talk to her nosey ass. She was the last person I wanted to talk to. If you want to know about anyone's business in this building, go to her, and she will hook you right on up.

"How is Dylan? Because I heard one of the concierge managers say that he hasn't been himself lately. So, you may wanna take him to see his doctor." She said as she started walking with me to the garage area of the building.

"Don't worry about him. He did go through a rough patch, but he's coming around now." I told her, hoping that she would be satisfied with my answer and haul ass in the direction she was going before she saw me.

"Okay, well that's good to hear. But know that if you guys need something just let Jimmy and I know."

"I will and thank you so much." I pretended like she was being gracious.

The moment Molly turned around to leave I pushed the door to the garage open and made a beeline for my car. I looked behind me at least five times, wondering if Dylan knew I had left the apartment. It wouldn't surprise me if he was still in the bathroom or in our bedroom, thinking that I was still in the house.

I know one thing, he's about to have a rude awakening.

Once I was in my car, I backed out of my parking space and then I quickly drove away. Upon exiting the parking garage I realized that I forgot my cell phone. Now how the fuck did I manage to do that? I know when Dylan finally tries to get in touch with me and hears my cell phone ringing inside of the apartment, he is going to flip out. I would pay money to see his facial expression because he's going to be freaking livid.

Fuck What You Heard!

KIRA

Since I really didn't have any plans, I decided to go shopping. Shopping has always been therapeutic for me so that's where I am going today. After I grab me a few expensive pieces from my favorite designers I'm going to also go by my father's bank so I can get his accounts transferred over to mine.

The thought of inheriting all of his possessions has a bittersweet affect on me. I pray that my father's death doesn't hunt me forever. I've seen it on TV where kids kill their parents everyday over money. Some of them get caught and some of them don't. The ones that get caught go to prison for life while the others grow old and are constantly reminded of their misdeeds, which inadvertently cause them sleepless nights. I'm not sure how my life will play out but I know that whatever comes my way I will have to deal with it. So hopefully, I will be ready.

As I headed in the direction of the mall, I decide to stop by my favorite store, Neiman

Marcus. They always have the latest fashion wear for me. My go-to-contact person at this location was Moreen. Moreen was a Hispanic woman. The first time I met her she told me that she was from Venezuela. She was a middle age woman and she new what was hot and what was not.

She greeted me as soon as I stepped foot into her department. "Hi Kira, how are you?" She asked, giving me smiles for days.

"I'm good Moreen, how are you?"

"I'm okay, now that you showed up." She said as she stood before me. Moreen resembled JLo. She was so stylish.

"Show me everything that just came in." I told her.

"Well, follow me this way." She insisted and then she took about ten steps to the right and I followed her. We ended up in the Givenchy section. Moreen showed me everything in the collection from the Geode Floral Dress to the Zip Waist Stretch Jacket with the High Waist Jeans. She even showed me the One-Sleeve Tunic Dress and I have to admit that I loved it. So, I asked her to pull my size in that dress and throw in the Zip Waist Jacket and the jeans. I also grabbed a Gucci pea coat and a leather bustier dress with leather flowers. When I concluded my shopping my tab came up to a little over $17,000. After I gave Moreen my American Express credit card, she took it and disappeared in the backroom. She reappeared three minutes later with my receipt and my clothes folded and packaged neatly in my shopping bags. "Thank you so much." I said.

"No, thank you for stopping by." Moreen replied and then she handed me her business card. I stuck it in my back pocket and then I exited the store.

When I approached the valet station outside Neiman Marcus I handed the Asian valet attendant my ticket and he grabbed my car keys from the locked box behind the stand and then he jogged around the corner to retrieve my car. He showed back up less than a minute later with my car in tow. After he hopped out of the driver seat, he stood there and held the door open for me. "Thank you so much," I said and handed him a $10 bill.

"Thank you ma'am." The valet driver replied after he helped me into my car. And as soon as I sat down in the driver seat he closed the door behind me. I drove off a second or two later. I looked at the time on the dashboard and realized that I had only been out for an hour. I knew I wasn't ready to go back home, so I headed on over to my father's bank so I could activate the transfer of his liquid cash and personal property.

The drive to Bank of Trust took me less than 10 minutes to get there. Immediately after I parked my car I looked in the rearview mirror so I could give my lips a little touchup of lipstick. I also used my fingers to toy with my hair and once I was satisfied with my look I grabbed my handbag that contained my father's important documents inside and then I stepped out of my car. When I turned around to close my door I panicked because everything went pitch black. And when I was swooped up by my waist and thrown down onto a hard surface, I screamed because I knew then that I had just gotten a satchel thrown over my head and that I was being kidnapped. "Please don't hurt me!" I screamed.

"Shut the fuck up bitch!" I heard a man's voice say.

"I've got money. Do you want money?" I managed to say while sobbing. I wanted to let this guy know that I was willing to do anything to be let go. But he wasn't hearing it.

"If you say another word I am going to put a slug in your head now." The guy roared. His voice boomed.

I tried to register that voice in my head, to see if I had heard it before but I couldn't. Whoever this was wasn't playing games. He sounded like he meant business so I laid there on a carpeted floor and remained quiet.

The drive seemed to take long. I tried to count the number of stops and turns we made to get an idea of where we were going, but I lost track of his driving pattern. And I believe it was done purposefully.

"Call 'K' and let 'em know we got her." I heard the guy say to someone else.

"I'm on it." The other guy replied.

When I heard the other guy speak I instantly analyze his voice too because I knew I had heard it somewhere else. "Come on Kira, think." I mumble to myself. And then that's when it hit me. The voice I just heard was from the same guy who threatened me at the elevator in my apartment building a while ago. "Oh shit! He works for Kendrick." I mumbled to myself again.

"Shut the fuck up!" The same guy snapped and before I knew it he punched me in the back of my head. The blow hit me really hard. The pain struck me like a lightening bolt. I saw stars even though I was still in the darkness.

"Ouuwwch," I screamed in agony.

"Bitch, scream again and see what I do!" The same guy warned me.

Believing that he would do as he said, I muffled my cry even in this excruciating pain. So, while I tried to suppress my agony I began to give myself yet another pep talk. *Kira, just try to remain calm so you can find a way to get out of this.*

"A yo' 'K', we just picked her up and now we're heading your way." I heard the other guy said.

I knew 'K' meant, Kendrick but I couldn't hear Kendrick's voice. I also knew that if I was being delivered to Kendrick, something isn't right. He has always warned me about this day, so what could it be about? My heart started beating erratically and not knowing why I was being taken to Kendrick was killing me on the inside. Right now would've been a perfect time to have my cell phone. But no, I had to leave it back at fucking apartment. Ugh! Now how was Dylan going to know what happen to me? And how was he going to be able to use the GPS on my phone to find out my location? I swear, I really fucked up this time.

Finally after driving in circles it seemed like, the vehicle stopped and before I could take a deep breath, I was dragged out of it. "You're hurting me. Somebody help!" I yelled. It didn't matter if I got hit this time because I was outside of the vehicle and I knew that this was my only chance to bring attention to what these clowns were doing to me.

"You can holler all you want you dumb bitch! Ain't no body gonna hear you because we're inside of a garage." He told me.

Stunned by his confession, I fell silent. And that's when I heard the garage door closing. After it hit the ground, my heart stopped. "Please let me go," I started begging. "I can give you whatever you want. Just don't kill me." I continued to plead with these guys.

"Good, I'm glad to hear that because we will be giving your boyfriend a call in just a few minutes." I heard another voice say. And at that very moment, I knew that voice came from Kendrick.

The guy holding me sat me down into a wooden chair and started wrapping duct tape around my wrists and my ankles. "Kendrick just tell me what you want and I'll make sure

Dylan give it to you." I assured him, while my head was still covered by the black satchel.

"Now that's what I wanna hear." He replied in a demonic like manner. I swear, I hated this guy but right now I was at his mercy so I was going to do whatever I needed to stay alive. "But what I wanna know is, why did you lie to me?" He continued and then he snatched the satchel from my head.

The sudden light blinded me for a moment so I had to readjust my eyes. I blinked them a few times and then I was finally able to see clearly. "What are you talking about?" I asked him. I swear, I had no idea what this guy was talking about.

"You told me that the cops didn't ask about me when they made you go down there and talk to them."

"And they didn't." I interjected.

"Shut the fuck up! I'm not done." He huffed. "You told me that my name never came up when they wanted to know who murdered that judge and his wife."

"It didn't." I lied, as fear started to consume my entire body. Yes, Detective Grimes did ask me if Kendrick had something to do with those murders but I couldn't tell

Kendrick that. I knew I had to stick to my story or this meeting isn't going to end right.

"Well then, why is the streets saying that you ratted me out?"

"I don't know." I continued to play the naïve role.

"Kira, everybody in the streets is saying that you ratted me out and told those cops everything. They even said that the reason why Dylan got out of jail was because you told the cops that I was the one that put the hit out on your pops, when in reality you and that nigga Nick did it."

"They are lying." I continued to look as convincing as possible.

"Kira, shut the fuck up!" Kendrick said and then he back-handily smacked me across my face. WAM! The blow stung me hard but I blocked out the pain. "Do you think that I don't know you're trying to get rid of me so Dylan can take over the streets? Do you think that I'm that stupid to believe that you didn't rat me out? Bitch, you're a fucking scammer! And I'm going to finish you and your boyfriend's ass tonight. So, get your soul right with God!" He continued and then he asked one of the guy's to hand him the disposal cell phone. The guy that drove me here handed Kendrick the phone. "Is this the new one?" Kendrick asked him.

"Yeah, I picked it up right before he grabbed her." He explained to Kendrick.

"Give me your boyfriend's number." Kendrick demanded.

Without hesitation I said, "555-8721.

I watched as Kendrick dialed Dylan's cell phone number. Right after it started ringing, Kendrick put the call on speaker. "Yo' who this?" I heard Dylan ask.

"I gotcha' bitch!" Kendrick told Dylan. His voice sounded sadistic.

"Who the fuck is this?" Dylan roared.

"Nigga, you know who it is. Now get your dough together because you're gonna need it to get your pretty little wifey back." Kendrick told him.

"Kendrick, I swear man if you put your motherfucking hands on my girl, I'm gonna kill you slow you fucking bitch ass nigga!" Dylan threatened.

"I'll tell you what, bring me $250,000 for your bitch. And if you wanna get into some gangsta shit, then we can do that too. And you only got one hour to do it." Kendrick warned him.

"Fuck you nigga! Don't put your fucking hands on her. I fucking mean it!" Dylan started ranting. He sounded like he was drunk, but then again, I couldn't tell. I only hoped that he gets here quickly with the money.

"Man, I ain't trying to hear all of that. Meet me at the 5261 Coastal Drive in one hour. Or your bitch dies!" Kendrick said and then he disconnected the call. He stuck the cell phone down into his front pants pocket and said, "Let's lock and load. No one lives out of here alive but us."

When Kendrick just said that only he and his boys are going to leave out of here alone, a dark cloud loomed over me. And at that point, something on the inside of me convinced me to believe him. Maybe I was taking my last breath today.

Calling For Help!!!

DYLAN

My mind raced like crazy after hanging up with that nigga, Kendrick. How the fuck did he kidnap Kira? Where the fuck was she when he snatched her up? I needed some answers and the frustrating part about all of this was that no one was around to answer them.

I immediately called Nick because what I was about to get into would require me to have him come along. "What's up Dee?" He asked me as soon as he answered his cell phone.

"Kendrick got Kira." I blurted out. I didn't know how else to say it.

"What the fucking are you talking about?" Nick asked me. He was acting like I was acting when Kendrick first uttered those words to me.

"Kendrick just called me and told me that he's got Kira and the only way I'm going to get her back is if I bring him $250,000."

"Do you have it?" Nick wanted to know.

"I'm short $50,000."

"Say no more. I'm coming to you right now." Nick told me.

"Nah, don't come here. Meet me at the Mc. Donald's near Coastal Drive because he's got her in one of those abandon houses around the corner from it."

"A'ight, I'm on my way now." Nick assured me.

"A'ight, so I'll see you then." I replied and then I ended the call.

I raced to my walk-in closet because that's where I had the $200,00 stashed. I was saving this money for a rainy day or one day when I decided that I was going to walk away from all the illegal shit I've done in the streets. I guess, the rainy day came before the day I retired from hustling.

The money was wrapped up in Saran Wrap to compress it. So when I pulled it from compartment in the closet ceiling, I looked at it and shook my head back and forth. I couldn't believe that I was about to depart with this money. It seemed like yesterday when I first started saving it. Bu it's all good because I'm going to get it back. With the money Kira is inheriting from her father, we're going to be right back on top.

I was a little drunk when I first got the phone call from Kendrick but I quickly sobered up after he dropped that bombshell on me. My only objective was to get my baby back. I just lost my mother and sister so I can't lose her too. No! That's not going to happen. Not today! Not ever!

I got in my car and threw the money onto the passenger seat of my car. When I hopped on the expressway I went from 35 mph. to 80 mph. in a matter of 3 seconds. I needed to hurry up and get Kira out of that situation. I know she's scared. And that burns me up inside. I don't want her experiencing anything like that. I'm supposed to be in her life to protect and take care of her. Not scream on her and let another nigga put his hands on her. What kind of mess is that? I've got some changing to do and I'm going to start it right after I get her back.

While I headed in the direction of the Mc. Donald's all I could think about was how Kira was acting? And how Kendrick was treating her? Then I wondered if she was already dead? "Damn, why didn't I ask to hear her voice?" I sucked my teeth. That's what a person paying the ransom does. I swear I hope she's still alive. I need to see her and feel her body against mine. If Kendrick has done something to her, I'm going to kill that motherfucker slowly. And then I'm going to kill his family next.

Nick was already parked at the Mc. Donald's when I pulled up. When I pulled into the parking lot Nick stepped out of his truck and got into my car. He pulled the money from the inside of his jacket pocket and handed it to me. "Man, I sure appreciate this." I told him.

"Listen Dee, you ain't gotta do that. We're family and I'll do anything for you. So, what's the plan?"

"He told me to come to the house up the street so that's what I am going to do."

"Do you think he's going to try to ambush you?" Nick wanted to know.

"I don't know, but I know he's gonna have his boys with him."

"Look Dee, we gotta do this thing right man. I wish we had more time to call in our boys because you just can't go in there and give that nigga $250,000 and think he's going to take it and everything is going to be cool after that. Trust me, Kendrick wants to get the money first and then he's going to try to kill you right after that."

"Yeah, I feel you."

"So, did he let you talk to Kira?"

"Nah, I was so mad that he called me talking shit that I didn't even think to ask him to let me talk to her."

"Come on Dylan, you no better than that man. What if you go there and she's already dead?"

"Nah, I can't bring myself to believe that."

"Well, you're gonna have to be a little smarter the next time."

"There ain't gonna be a next time." I told him.

"Cool! Enough said," Nick commented and then he said, "Check this out, let's go there in separate cars. You pull up in the front and I go in from the side. And if that nigga tries something then we're gonna blast our way out of that place."

"All right, let's do it." I agreed.

The Rescue Mission

KIRA

"Think that nigga is gonna bring the money?" One of Kendrick's boys asked Kendrick.

"What kind of question is that? Of course he is. He loves this pretty young thang!" Kendrick commented and then he walked over to where they had me duct taped to the chair and kissed me on the forehead.

I yanked my head back. "Don't fucking touch me!" I hissed. I was disgusted by the mere touch of his lips.

"Whatcha' mean don't touch you? I thought we were friends?" Kendrick joked as he stood before me.

"Friends don't hurt friends or threaten to kill them." I replied.

"Well, I'm a different kind of friend. See, I'm the kind of friend that will give you the world one day and kill you the next."

"That's not a friend. That's a fucking psycho!"

"I wasn't a psycho when I used to come to the dealership and spend hundreds of thousands of dollars. You were all smiles then."

"Yeah, that was before I found out that you used me to get my father's friend's home address."

"Well, everything would've gone perfectly if your father would've stay out of their business."

"What about Nancy? You didn't have to kill her."

"I have my own reasons for that situation."

"Do you even have a conscious?"

"I've got a conscious. But do you? I mean, it's not like your hands are clean. You did murder your pops, right?"

"I didn't do shit." I denied. I refused to let Kendrick put me in the same category with him. I murdered my father so not only could Dylan win his case and get released from jail, I also did it because I could've been implicated too.

The guy that threw me into the van chuckled and said, "K, I think she's lying."

"I think so too." Kendrick said and then he smiled.

"Look at the way she's looking at you 'K', I think she might have a thing for you." The driver commented.

"I think you might be right." Kendrick replied and then he leaned towards me and tried to give me another kiss.

"Didn't I say don't fucking kiss me? Your lips feels nasty." I spat.

"Damn 'K,' she's being real disrespectful right now." The driver point out.

"Shut the fuck up you fucking street hustler! You don't know shit about me." I snapped.

"Bitch, you don't know shit about me either!" He snapped back.

"I know enough to know that you're gonna always be Kendrick's flunky. He ain't gonna ever let you make no real money. He's gonna keep you and this clown in True Religion jeans and Jordan's until your dumb asses get locked up. And then you ain't gonna hear from him anymore because he's gonna turn his back on you. And before you know it, you're gonna be put in a jail cell with a big, black, ugly nigga name Bubba and he's gonna call you his bitch!"

Kendrick burst into laughter. "Now, that was funny!

"I see those clowns that work for you don't think so."

"Bitch, shut up! The driver continued.

"Yeah, I'll shut up when you grow some balls." I said sarcastically.

"Kendrick, let me hit that bitch in her mouth a couple of times." The driver begged.

"Nah, just chill. You'll get your chance with her. After we kill her punk ass boyfriend, I'm gonna let y'all rape her boujee ass!"

"Oh so y'all are into raping women now. Can't get pussy any other way?" I said calmly, even though I was scared out of my mind.

"Put some tape over that bitch mouth!" Kendrick barked.

The driver grabbed the duct tape and tore a huge piece from it. I tried moving my head, making it difficult for him to place the tape over my mouth but it didn't work. After he managed to get the tape on, he looked at me said, "I think she looks cute like that, huh?"

"Just perfect!" Kendrick agreed, while the other guy laughed.

The Set Up

DYLAN

The house of 5261 Coastal Drive looked like a crack house spot. All of the windows were boarded up and the grass surrounding the house looked like a wheat field. The grass was at least 8 feet tall. Before I stepped out of my car, I made sure my pistol was tucked securely in the waist of my jeans. I also made sure that the envelope with the money inside was secured in my back pocket too. I took a deep breath and then I exhaled. "Come on Dylan, it's either do or die." I mumbled to myself and then I took the first step towards the front door of this run down shack.

I knew I was being watched when the front door opened as I made my way onto the porch. When I got a closer look I recognized the guy to be Omar. Omar was a young kid from Pork & Beans project. He's been working trap houses for Kendrick for sometime now. It's no shock to see him here though. I hear in the streets that his little kid has heart and he ain't afraid to lose it either. "Nigga, is you scrapped?" He asked me.

"Nigga, fuck you! Respect your elders." I barked at him. I wanted to send the message to him that I'm an Old 'G' out here and that he needs to respect me.

"Man, I ain't trying to hear that shit. Give me your piece nigga or you ain't getting in here."

I hesitated for a second trying to figure out what to do. I didn't want to give this little young boy my only pistol. I'd be committing suicide if I did that. So, while I contemplated on what to do, I heard Kendrick's voice coming from inside the old house. "Let 'em in." He said, even though I couldn't see him.

"You heard him little nigga! Now get out of my way." I huffed.

"Fuck you!" Omar said and then he gritted on me.

"Yo' Kendrick, tame your little man and tell him to get out of my way." I yelled through the front door. "I don't feel confortable with him walking behind me." I continued.

"Omar, move back so he can come in." Kendrick instructed him.

"You heard him little boy! Get the fuck out of my way." I snarled at him. The guy

Omar finally moved out of my way so I could get into the front door. Kendrick instructed him to stand at least 5 feet away while we made the exchange. So, when I walked into the room I saw another guy with Kendrick. His face was familiar but I couldn't tell you his name. And when I continued to look around the room I finally saw Kira. I almost came to tears when I saw her duct taped to a chair with her mouth covered too. I could tell that she was crying too. She also looked relieved that I was there.

"So, where is the money?" Kendrick didn't hesitate to ask.

I looked around the entire room just so I could get a clear look at my way of escape just in case Kendrick wanted to try some underhanded shit. "I got it. But I'm gonna need you to let her go first."

"Nah, that's not how it's going to go down. You're gonna give me the money first and then I'm gonna let her go." Kendrick wouldn't budge.

"Well, then we ain't gonna be able to make the trade." I stalled him. I knew Nick was somewhere around but I didn't know where. I needed a sign.

"Listen you little whack as nigga! This is my kidnap victim so you're gonna have to go by my rules."

"Okay wait, do you want me to go back outside and try this shit again. Because if we keep going back and forth like this, then we ain't gonna be able to accomplish anything." I suggested. But Kendrick wasn't hearing it. He was pissed. He was so pissed that he pulled out his pistol and aimed it at me.

"See, I was trying to be nice but you just had to push my button." He began to say, "I'm not here to accommodate you and your bitch! I'm here to collect my $250,000, which I have yet to see. But not only that, I'm here to set the record straight because I've been hearing some snitch shit in the streets."

"What the fuck are you talking about?" I asked him. I was curious to know what he was referring to.

"Oh nigga, don't act like you didn't know that your bitch here told the cops that I killed the judge, his wife and that girl that used to work with her. She even told them that I killed her pops too so she could get your clown ass a get-out-of-jail free card. But we all know the truth about who killed her daddy, don't we?"

"I don't know what you're talking about." I said.

"Dee, don't play games with me. I know you got her to snitch me out so I can get locked up and you take over the streets. But that ain't gonna happen." Kendrick said, as he walked closer to me.

I felt the sweat pouring out of my pores as I watched Kendrick walk slowly towards me. I was trying to figure out how I was going to pull my gun from my waist and aim it at him before he got any closer. I knew the timing had to be right or else Kira and I was going to be carried out of here in body bags.

While Kendrick talked his way into my direction, my boy Nick came up from behind Omar and aimed his pistol at Omar's head. "Nigga, don't you move!" Nick said.

After everyone heard Nick's voice in the room, they turned their focus on him.

"Oh so, you had to bring in reinforcements, huh?" Kendrick commented.

"You know how the game plays." Nick interjected.

"So, how we gonna do this?" I asked Kendrick because I was ready to get Kira and get the fuck out of here before these niggas get trigger-happy.

Crooked Cops

KIRA

While Kendrick tried to gather his thoughts and try to keep up the notion that he was still in charge of this situation everyone in the room heard another voice.

"Bravo! Bravo!" Detective Grimes said, clapping his hands as he and Detective Brady walks casually into the room. "I see my plan worked out perfectly." He continued as he and Detective Brady approached everyone in the room. Detective Brady had his police issued firearm aimed at Kendrick's two henchmen.

"What the fuck is going on? What kind of plan?" Dylan blurted out.

"You fucking drug dealers believe everything you hear on the streets." Detective Grimes started off saying, "So, all I had to do was get my informant to spread a rumor that Kira was feeding information to me and my colleagues about Kendrick and his crew moving a lot drugs and they were the ones who murdered Judge Mahoney and his wife. And I knew this would be believable because everything I just said was the truth. Kira's father gave us everything we needed. The only thing that stopped us from securing indictments was the fact that we needed confirmation. We needed another person to confirm the information Mr. Wade gave us, but Kira wouldn't budge one bit. But thank God for GPS and recording devices because not only did we find out that Dylan wanted to murder Kendrick for the continuous threats against Kira, Dylan also wanted to get rid of you Kendrick because of conflicts dealing with drug turfs. So I figured why not get these two in a room together? In my mind, one of two things are going to happen, they're going to kill each other or they're going to rat on one another and I'm going to get it all on tape. Smart move, huh?"

"You set us up?" Kendrick roared, his voice boomed like a lion while he held firmly onto his pistol.

Detective Grimes chuckled. "You made it so easy to do."

I couldn't say a word with the duct tape covering my mouth. But Dylan and Nick had a lot to say while they kept their pistols aimed at both Kendrick and his two homeboys. "You dumb motherfuckers brought the cops here!" Dylan cursed, spitting venom from his mouth.

"I'm not going to jail. I'll die first." Nick said, his voice trembled a little.

"Everyone just stay calm." Detective Grimes uttered as he tried to walk closer. Detective Brady stayed behind him with his gun aimed in the direction of Kendrick and his boys.

"Fuck staying calm! Just let me take Kira and we'll go." Dylan said.

"Yeah, fuck that! Let us leave and you can do whatever you want with them!" Nick interjected.

"I'm sorry but that's not going to happen." Detective Grimes announced.

"So you think you're gonna take all of us to jail?" Kendrick's voice boomed.

"Yeah cracker! You think you and that motherfucker behind you is going to take all of us down?" One of Kendrick's boys said, with his finger on the trigger.

I've got to admit that I was really afraid at what was about to happen. Almost everyone around me had a gun in their hands and I was in the center of it all. With a one-shot I could die instantly. And no one will be able to bring me back. So what do I do? Just sit here and listen to these trigger-happy ass niggas debate back and forth about who's going to throw up the white flag and who's not? This was no place for me. I'm not supposed to be here. But unfortunately I am, so what do I do now?

"Listen you guys, let's end this thing peacefully. I don't want to see anybody die or being hauled off to the emergency room. So, do the right thing and put your gun down on the ground." Detective Grimes suggested.

"Fuck you! I'm not doing shit!" Kendrick yelled. "And I'm definitely not putting my pistol down on the ground. But I am going to count to three and if you don't put your pistol down on the ground or turn around so me and my boys can leave then its gonna be a blood bath up in here."

"Yeah nigga, you tell your partner to put his gun down so I can get my lady and leave or shit is gonna get really ugly in here." Dylan added.

"Wait! Hold up! Let's talk this thing out." Detective Grimes interjected.

"Nah, fuck that! You've said enough." Kendrick huffed and then he started counting. "One," and before he said the number two, Detective Brady fired off three rounds, hitting Kendrick and Dylan. I saw Dylan fall to the floor first and Kendrick fell down on the floor next. My heart took a huge plunge down to the pit of my stomach. I wanted to scream but I couldn't. I wanted to get out of this chair so I could pull Dylan to safety but I couldn't. I watched as Detective Brady continued to fire his gun from around the wall he found and used it as refuge. Nick found himself a spot behind a door that led to another room. And when I looked at Detective Grimes, Dylan and Kendrick all three of them were lying motionless on the floor. I swear I was about to lose my fucking mind. "Dylan get up!" I screamed, but my words were muffled as the tears started falling down my face. "Baby, please get up!" I screamed once again, my words were muffled.

By this time, my face was saturated with my tears. I couldn't see anything out of my eyes at this point. Everything around me was blurred. But I could see sparks coming from the barrel of the guns and I could see motions from the bodies moving around me. And when I tuned in to listen to what was going on, I heard Detective Brady say, "Officer down! We need paramedics now."

"What's your location?" I heard a female dispatcher say.

"We're at 5261 Coastal Drive. We are in a dilapidated house in a cul-de-sac. Please hurry. The officer has been shot." Detective Brady explained. And when I looked in the direction of where Detective Brady's voice was coming from, I realized that he was still using that wall as refuge and that he had managed to pull Detective Grimes around that wall with him. "Hold on Grimes, you're gonna be fine. But you have to stay with me." Detective Brady continued.

Listening to Brady give Detective Grimes a pep talk led me to believe that Grimes was on his last leg. And hearing this made me turn my focus back to Dylan. Unlike Grimes, Dylan wasn't moving. "Baby, get up!" I said but my words were still muffled. I knew he couldn't hear me so I sat there and watched him closely. And suddenly from the corner of my eye I saw movement, but that movement came from Nick. He startled the hell out of me sneaking up behind me. But then again, I was happy to see him. "Keep quiet, so I can get you out of here." He instructed me while he ripped away the duct tape from my wrists and ankles. Immediately after I was freed from that chair I started pulling the duct tape from my mouth while Nick tended to Dylan.

Nick tried to move Dylan but he was unresponsive. After I got the tape from around my mouth I rushed over to Dylan's side. "What's wrong with him?" I whispered to Nick.

"He's dead." Nick told me as he searched underneath Dylan's shirt. A second or two later Nick found what he was looking for. And when I looked at it, I knew that instant that that was the ransom money.

But I wasn't listening to him. I reached for Dylan's head so I could lift him up while the tears continued to fall from my eyes.

"Kira, we have to go now." Nick hissed and then he pushed my hands back from Dylan's head. "Let's go." He continued as he pulled me up from the floor.

I tried to break away from Nick's grasp but he was too strong. And to make sure I couldn't fight him anymore, he threw me over his shoulders so he could carry me out of the house. As he carried me towards the exit door, I heard Detective Brady trying desperately to keep Detective Grimes alive. "Come on, Grimes… the paramedics will be here any minute so hold on." I heard Detective Brady saying.

Then my attention shifted to Kendrick who I knew was dead for sure. When he fell after Brady shot him, his homeboys fled the scene. They left him lying in a pool of his own blood. Kendrick didn't have a fighting chance. He is gone and never coming back. I knew I only had a few seconds left to get another look at Dylan before my window of opportunity was gone. Nick was walking pretty fast so I focused my eyes on his face. His eyes were open so I tried not to think of him being dead. I looked at him like he was gazing off into the sky. I wanted to remember him for the good he had done in my life. Not the Dylan who had been verbally abusive to me these last week and a half. That Dylan, I wanted to forget.

After Nick exited the abandon house with my thrown over his shoulder, he put me down so I could walk the rest of the way to the car. But before I took the first step a sudden wind brushed across my face and I had to catch my breath. I stood there for a moment to process what had just happened, until I heard sirens blaring in the night air. "Come on Kira, we gotta' go." Nick urged me and took off running. I followed suit. Immediately after I jumped into Nick's truck, he drove into an alley behind the house to avoid running into the paramedics and cops that were coming in the opposite direction. So, as he drove away, I turned around and looked back at the house one more time and whispered the words, I love you to Dylan.

"You talking to me?" Nick asked.

"No, I was talking to myself." I replied and turned back around in my seat.

"You know we're gonna have to leave town, right?" He informed me.

"And go where?" I asked him.

"Somewhere far from here." He said and then he pressed down on the accelerator and sped off into the night.

Sneak Peek into:
"The Score"
(E-book & Paperback Available Right Now)

Prologue

LAUREN

Present Day

My feet moved at the speed of lightening. I could feel the wind beating on my skin so it made snot wet the inside of my nostrils. My entire body was covered with a thick sheen of sweat and I could feel it burning my armpits. My breath escaped my mouth in jagged, raggedy puffs and the inside of my nostrils stung. My chest also burned and my heart felt like it would burst through the front of it. Even feeling as terrible as I did, I would not and could not stop moving to make it stop.

"Move!"

"Get out of my fucking way!"

"Watch out!"

"Move!"

I screamed command after command at the nosey ass people that were staring and gawking and being in my damn in my way. My legs were moving like those of a swift and agile cheetah as I swerved and swayed through the throngs of people on Virginia Beach Boulevard. I was met by more than one mouthful of gasps and groans and I could faintly see more than one wide-eyed, mouth-agape stare as people gawked at me like I was a crazy woman. I guess I did look crazy running through the high-end shopping area with no shoes on (I had run straight out my Louboutins), my expensive embellished Balmain skirt hitched up around my hips, my vixen weave blowing in the wind and my Chanel caviar bag strapped around my arm like a slave chain. I could also tell that my makeup was a cakey, smudged mess all over my face and eyes. I could only imagine how ghastly I looked at that moment. I didn't give a damn. I wasn't going to stop running no matter what. Looking crazy was the least of my worries. My main focus was on trying to get way so I was still moving nonstop. My mouth was cotton ball dry and I was so thirsty my throat felt like I had swallowed a sword of fire.

I had run track in high school and it was still paying off now, but clearly I wasn't in the same athletic shape. Still, I wasn't about to go out like this. I wasn't going to get captured on the street and probably murdered for something that wasn't totally my fault. I had been pushed and provoked to do everything that I did. All of the mistakes. All of the grimy shit I had done over the years. All of it was because I was born at a disadvantage from day fucking one.

I didn't want to die. I had always saw myself growing old with a few kids and grandkids surrounding me when I was ready to be settled. I would've given anything to be old and settled at this moment, but of course, life threw me a curb ball.

Even on concrete I could hear the thunderous footfalls of the three men that were chasing me. I think if they weren't so damn gorilla big and slower than me they would have caught me.

"Hey! Are you ok?" I heard a man on the street yell at me as I flew past him nearly knocking him over. Why the hell was he asking

me such a dumb question when you could clearly see that I was being chased by three hulking goons dressed in all black with their guns probably showing on their waists or maybe even in their hands. Thank goodness I am always so alert or they would've walked right up on my while I unsuspectingly ate my lunch at the posh restaurant and grabbed me. It was the fact that I had only been back in town for a few hours, the eeriness of my missing date and the suspicious looks that had alerted me in the first place. How could I have been so trusting? So naïve and stupid too.

I could feel the look of terror contorting my face, so I know damn well passersby could see the fear etched on every inch of it.

Finally, I dipped through a side alley and the first door I tried allowed me inside. Thank God! With my chest heaving up and down I rested my back against another cold metal door inside and slid down to the floor. My legs were still trembling and my muscles were on fire in places on my body I didn't even know existed. I tried to slow down my rapid breathing so I could hear whether the men had noticed me dipping into the alley but the more I tried to calm myself the more reality set in about the grave danger I was in. I was probably about to be murdered or worse tortured and then murdered right in a dank alleyway in the place I thought I would never return to. If I hadn't gotten that call it would have been years before I crept back here. I thought about Matt and wondered if he was the one who had sent these men after me. But how would he have known I was back? I knew Matt had a lot of selfish ways about him and although shit had gone south with us, I never thought he would try to do something like this to me. I expected that if he wanted to confront me, he would come himself. Even if it was Yancy that had sent the goons, I would think Matt would have tried to spare me.

CLANG!

A loud noise outside interrupted my thoughts and caused me to jump. I clasped both of my hands over my mouth and forced the scream that had crept up my throat back down. Sweat trickled down my face and burned my eyes. My heart jack hammered against my chest bone so hard it actually hurt. My stomach knotted up so tightly the cramps were almost unbearable. I dropped my head. Suddenly I felt like vomiting.

"I don't see her! She's not down here!" I heard one of the goons outside of the door

scream to the others. I swallowed hard and started praying under my breath.

Dear God, I am sorry for all of the things I've done. I don't know how things got so far gone. I never meant anything by any of it. I just wanted to live a better life than I had as a child. I guess the mother you gave me and the hand you dealt me I should've just handled it. I should've worked harder and not try to take the easy way out all of the time. I know stealing is wrong. Since the first time I stole a credit card from my foster mother's purse, who was bank manager, I knew it was wrong, but I got addicted to the since that I had gotten over on someone. I felt powerful. I remember the times I'd hear her talking to my foster father about some of the frauds scams she witnessed by working at the bank. It was interesting to hear how bank and credit card frauds were being committed on a daily basis. To hear the stories were intoxicating. I had to test the waters and here I am today. I'm literally running for me life. And where is Matt when I needed him. He was supposed to be the person who saved me. But instead, he hurt me more than anything. Maybe this is your way of teaching me a lesson. Trust me, I hear you loud and clear. If you let me get out of this, I swear I will change my life. I don't even know how things got this far...

Those last few words of my prayer resonated with me the longest. I truly didn't know how I had gotten to this point. I immediately started to think back on everything that had happened...

MATT

"Ooof," I gagged as another fist slammed into my diaphragm causing all of the wind in my body to involuntarily escape through my mouth. Acidy vomit leapt up into my throat and spew out of my mouth right after.

"Hit that bitch ass nigga again!" a deep baritone voice commanded. With that, another sledgehammer sized fist slammed into my left jaw. I felt the blood and spit shoot from between my lips. The salt from the blood stung the open cuts on my split bottom lip.

"Until he tells me where the fuck every dime of my money is I want his ass to suffer," the deep voice growled. "Break every bone in his body if you have to."

"Agh!" I belted out as a heavy booted foot crashed down on my ribcage. I think hearing the crack and crunch of my own bones disturbed me more than the excruciating pain I felt.

I coughed and wheezed trying to will my lungs to fill back up with air. Each raggedy breath hurt like hell. I knew then that some of my ribs had been shattered. More fury came right after.

"Ugh!" I coughed as a front kick with a pointed, steel toe boot slammed into my back. I swore I heard my spine crack. My insides felt like they were being shuffled around by the punches and kicks I'd been subjected to since these dudes had snatched me from my condo in the thick of the night. I had tried to bounce before they could get me, but I was too slow. Thank God, Lauren had up and left or else she would've been there when they broke the door down to get me. Although I wanted to kill her myself right now, I could only pray that she was some place safe…maybe with the police or back on the run. But if these niggas were after me, I would think they would be after her and Yancy as well.

"Where is my fucking money!" the voice boomed again. This time, I forced my battered eyes open and looked at the sharply dressed man that was standing over me. Flashing a sparkly diamond pinky ring, solid gold cufflinks and a clearly expensive tailor made suit, this nigga hadn't even broken a sweat. He obviously took great satisfaction in commanding his goons to torture me over and over. And like good little soldiers, they did just enough to hurt me, but not kill me.

"I'll ask you one more time Matthew Connors…what the fuck did you and your bitch do with my fucking money," the boss man growled. His money? Me and my bitch? What the…It finally hit me like a hammer to my head. My entire body went cold like my veins had been injected with ice water. I knew right then that I was in the clutches of Nikolai Romanov, a millionaire businessman in public but secretly one of the most dangerous hustlers in the entire United States. I had had envied Nick since the day I found out who he really was. Nick was one of those dudes I could've been like if shit didn't go south in my operation. Now, I hated niggas like him. He was a constant reminder of what I could've been if I didn't have snitch niggas in my circle that turned on me. Knowing it was Nick ordering my torture just incited more anger inside of me. Although my heart was galloping because I was clearly scared of Nick and his goons at the moment, the rage and pure jealousy in my brain made me spew a mouthful of blood and saliva in Nick's direction. I knew Nick's type. He wasn't in the business of giving mercy; especially to someone who he felt had crossed him. I figured Nick would kill me anyway so why tell him anything and why show him any respect. It was niggas like Nick that always shitted on small time hustlers like me and kept us from climbing from the slums to the boardroom like Nick had done. Call me a jealous, hating ass nigga if you want, I don't care, if I couldn't live like a high and mighty king no more, I didn't give a fuck about the niggas that did. He was going to have to kill me before I showed him an ounce of respect.

"F…Fu…Fuck you," I managed through battered lips. Each word was painful coming out, but I was a man with pride on top of everything.

Nick let out a raucous, maniacal laugh. "Oh you're a tough guy now? You petty fuckin' thief," He spat as he moved closer to me. "It's pieces of shit like you that make all of us look bad. Stealing instead of going out there and working for your own shit. I can respect a man that hustles for himself, but a man who steals from another hardworking man is a waste of fucking sperm. Your mother should've just swallowed," Nick hissed. The heat of anger that lit up my chest from his words was probably enough to make me kill him with my bare hands. I bucked my body out of anger but that just made shit worse.

"Aggh!" I screamed when Nick crushed one of his hard bottom Salvatore Ferragamo loafers down into my balls. The famous Ferragamo buckle glinted off the bright lights and taunted me. I guess this was payback for all of the times I had purchased expensive Ferragamo shit with other people's money and identities. Maybe Nick was right, a man who is a thief is the worst type of motherfucker alive.

"Now you little bitch. I want to know how you got the balls to steal my money and where it is now. I'm not going to keep playing so nice because this…this little bit of ass whooping and pain is nothing compared to what I do to niggas like you who I see as the scum of the earth," Nick growled. Then he stomped down on my balls with what felt like the force of a ten-ton boulder.

"Hmgh!" I screamed out and panted for breath at the same time. The pain was unbearable. I could barely catch my breath. Small squirms of light flitted through my eyes. I was literally seeing stars.

"That's what I thought. Now, if you want to make it out of this alive you better fucking start talking," Nick snarled. "You must've realized by now that you and your little female crew of thieves fucked with the wrong man," Nick hissed. "I just look like a normal wealthy businessman. You have no idea who I really am. Not even now."

"Agggh!!" I shrieked as the square heel of Nick's shoe slammed into my nuts again. This time with so much force I felt like my ball sack had busted open. I opened my battered and swollen eyes and stared up at the blinding light dangling from the ceiling. I was praying and inviting death to just come take me away from this pain. I could feel the walls closing in on me but before the darkness and the shock engulfed me I thought about Lauren and Yancy and all the shit we had done to get to this point. Suddenly I was thrust back in time to how all of this shit started….

LAUREN

<u>Six Months Earlier</u>

"I'll take two of those classics. The red and the royal blue patent leather," I leaned into the counter and pointed at two bags on the shelf behind it. "I think these are the only two I don't have in my collection," I chimed proudly. I could be a snob when I wanted to be. The Asian saleslady widened her slits-for-eyes at me but she tried to keep a smile on her face. I could tell she was probably secretly judging me and more than likely instantly thought I couldn't afford these expensive ass bags. It was amusing to me to watch her struggling to keep it professional because she also knew just as well as I did that my purchase of these two five-thousand dollar Chanel bags would be a pay load of commission for her.

As the snobby saleslady worked to retrieve my items, I kept shopping with my eyes. Now, I felt like I had a little point to prove. I smirked to myself and for spite I decided to make her piss her pants with jealousy. See, I had worked retail back in my day so I knew that no matter how stuck up these bitch salesladies acted, they were broke as hell and really silently prayed for the commission fairy to bless them. I bet when I walked in she had immediately looked at my race and pegged me as a window shopper and eye hustler. I was about to show this bitch how Lauren Kelly rolled.

"Wow, these are beautiful too. Hmmm, I think I should take every color of these as well," I said pointing down into the counter at the Chanel cuff bracelets. The saleswoman almost dropped the pocketbooks as she clamored over and grabbed the merchandise I was asking for with the quickness. I could hear the cash register in her head singing ching-ching. Jewelry sales always brought more commission than things that sold faster like pocketbooks. I chuckled to myself.

"Is that all?" she asked me.

"I think I've done enough damage for one day," I said snobbishly. Then I slapped the newly cloned Master Card I had down on the counter. The saleslady squinted at my card, picked it up and looked it over like it was a piece of shit. I could see disappointment in her face that my card wasn't American Express. I quickly began feeling indignant. *How dare this bitch!*

"Do you do that to all customers or just the black ones?" I asked through my teeth.

Her eyes popped wide like I had just dashed a cup of cold water in her face.

"I'm sure if I was a member of any other race you would have picked up my card with a smile and ran to the register. *Now,* do I need to take my business and my commission to another store?" I gritted. The threat was readily apparent in my tone.

The saleswoman's cheeks flushed deep red and she shifted her weight from one foot to the other. She parted a halfhearted, embarrassed smile and broke eye contact with me.

"No ma'am and I apologize if you feel that way," she replied meekly.

"That's what I thought, now ring me up or this store will be all over the eleven o'clock news when I'm done speaking to the media about the blatant discrimination I experienced here," I snapped. The petite, pancake-assed bitch raced to the small suite in the store where they ring purchases over a certain amount. I could tell I had scared the holy shit out of her, which is what I wanted to do. Luckily, my threat to go to the media and my forceful attitude was going to be a great distraction in case anything went wrong with the card. Those credit cards were always hit or miss, although, up to that point (knock on wood) they had always been complete out-of-the-park homeruns whenever I used them.

As I stood there waiting for her to return with my nicely bagged and wrapped items my cell phone buzzed inside of my Hermes Birkin bag. I looked at the screen and sucked my teeth. It was my boyfriend Matt. I wasn't feeling his ass right at that moment and hadn't been for the past few weeks. As far as I was concerned, he was a sneaky, conniving bastard that had it coming to him in the worse way. The only reason I even still fucked with him was because I had a plan that I needed to see come to fruition. I had just secretly found out that Matt and our other partner in crime Yancy had been fucking around behind my back. It was a complete blow to my brain and heart because of all of the people in the world; I had trusted those two with everything that I had, including, my heart. I had basically saved that bitch Yancy from a life of stealing and fucking men for money. After buying a bunch of stolen jewelry items from Yancy, I literally saved that bitch off the street and I got to know her well. I kind of felt sorry for her when she told me how rough she was having it out there selling her pussy with her crazy ass pimp down on her every fucking second of the day. Me being the thoughtful person that I am, offered to let Yancy in on my operation. At the time I was just starting to do the fake credit cards and check kiting after Matt had lost all his shit. I was the big breadwinner and Matt was living off of me. I gave Yancy a role in what we were doing and brought her around my man. Big fucking mistake. Yes, I knew Yancy was a pretty young girl who knew the art of seduction, but I thought loyalty would be as important to her as it was to me. Unfortunately, I was wrong.

Yancy was one of those video vixen types who wore a lot of weave, a lot of makeup and had the fake tits and ass implants. She stood five feet even without heels and about five feet six inches with heels on. She had a small waist, wide hips, and a beautiful smooth caramel skin complexion that I had always yearned for as a kid. I can't say that if I was a man like Matt I would not have been attracted to Yancy too, but I wouldn't be that grimy either. As long as I live I will never forget the day I first found out about them. Now, standing right in the Chanel store I couldn't stop the memory of what happened from crashing in on me…

July 2013

It was a hot ass, heat wave type of July day in the Tidewater area and I was flustered from a day of shopping. Sweat had my hair plastered to my head like I had gelled it down purposely. The twenty bags I was lugging had my body drenched in sweat and pain shot up my arms and down my back with each movement I made.

"Where the fuck is Matt when I need his ass?" I had huffed. I had called him like six times before I pulled into our condo parking garage. You would think that he would answer knowing that I had been out all day getting shit for us to resell in the hood. Sometimes he used our illegal enterprise to buy things to sell on the hot market for some quick and easy cash. It was better than keeping every material thing for our own personal use.

After struggling for ten minutes and fishing around in my oversized Gucci bag for another three minutes, I finally got my key out. I sat the bags down at my feet and put the key into the bottom lock of the condo I shared with Matt. At first the door wouldn't open. I crinkled my face in confusion and sucked my teeth. Then I realized why the door wasn't opening.

"Why the fuck did he lock the top lock? He knows we never do that," I grumbled. I pulled the key out of the bottom lock and shuffled through my key ring until I found the top lock key. I got the door open after a few minutes.

"Finally," I breathed out as the cool air from the air conditioner inside hit my face. I stepped inside and dragged my bags in after me. I think it was the music blasting and the type of music that hit me first.

"I can love you in the bedroom or on top of my water bed. On the patio...we can do it anywhere," 112 sang.

That was me and Matt's song when we first started dating. It still made me blush hearing it since he and I had made love for the first time with that song on repeat.

I smirked, immediately thinking that maybe he had planned something sweet like a romantic evening for us since we had been kind of at each other's throats days before.

With a huge, sexy grin on my face, I walked down the long hallway towards our bedroom. I was going to surprise him since I had busted in on him trying to surprise me. I kicked off my Giuseppe's and started unbuttoning my blouse. The closer I got to our bedroom door the more the music moved through my soul. I swayed my hips sexily practicing for the show I was planning to put on for Matt. I started to knock on the door, but I thought it would be sexier to catch Matt in the act of fixing up our room for my romantic surprise. I can't even lie, I was giddy inside for the first time in a long. Matt hadn't done anything like this in a long time because we had literally been fighting almost every day.

I finally made it down our long hallway and to the bedroom door. I was almost naked, standing there in just my lace La Perla bra and thong. I reached down to turn the doorknob and that's when I heard it. It was like a bomb had exploded in my ears.

"Ewww Matt. Oh yeah. Right there. Fuck me harder. Harder!" Even with the music blaring I recognized the voice as Yancy's. Then...

"Whose pussy is this? Call me daddy! Call me your fuckin' daddy!" I heard Matt growl. Those were words he had said to me exactly like he was saying them to that bitch. My mind was telling me to bust up in that room

and kill the both of them, but for some reason my body was not following directions.

I froze and my feet became rooted to the floor. A tornado of emotions swirled inside of me and I felt unsteady on my feet. Suddenly, I could no longer hear the music blasting and all could hear is the sound of lovemaking coming from MY bedroom. My heart rate sped up so fast it made my head swirl. I was suddenly unsteady on my feet. My first instinct was to bust in the room and go balistic on Matt and Yancy's ass. I wanted to fuck her up so badly that no one would recognize her face and cut his dick off so he'd never be able to use it again. My entire body was trembling and then I realized I was standing there half naked still in my underwear like the damn naïve fool that I was. The fucking joke was on me. Here I was thinking my man was surprising me with something sweet, instead; I surprised myself. Tears involuntarily rolled down my face before what was happening really registered in my brain. I snatched my hand back from the doorknob like it was on fire. Suddenly my body came alive with the heat of shame and embarrassment. You fucking fool! They've been playing you all along! I silently chastised myself.

I quickly scooped up my clothes and ran down the hallway to the front of the condo. With my chest heaving up and down and my entire body trembling like a leaf in a wild storm I slipped back into my clothes. Whirling around like I madwoman I located my purse, grabbed it and my cell phone and rushed back out the front door. I didn't know where I was going but I knew I had to get out of there before I caught a case. Stupid! Stupid! Stupid! I chanted in my head. How could I be that stupid not to know that Yancy and Matt had been fucking? No wonder my relationship with him was on the rocks.

In tears I raced to my car, got in and just started to drive aimlessly. I couldn't even think straight. At first, I thought about driving to my old neighborhood and buying a dirty gun, going back to the condo and shooting Yancy and Matt. Then, I thought about calling his probation officer and telling him all that Matt was into so Matt could get violated and sent back to prison. Then I thought about going to Yancy's little townhouse and setting that shit on fire. All sorts of things ran through my mind, but finally, after driving around for hours I came to a resolution that I felt wickedly good about.

"Y'all fucked around on the wrong bitch. I may be a lot of things, but stupid I am not," I growled out loud as if Matt and Yancy could hear me. At that moment, I had decided that instead of being ratchet and raising hell and acting like a classless chick, I would slowly and methodically plot my revenge. I decided that I would destroy Yancy and Matt slowly and watch their lives crumble to ashes, but not before I got everything I wanted out of the deal at their expense.